Over the End Line

Over the End Line

by *Alfred C. Martino*

HARCOURT

Houghton Mifflin Harcourt

Boston New York 2009

Harcourt is an imprint of Houghton Mifflin Harcourt Publishing Company.

www.hmhbooks.com

The text of this book is set in Garth Graphic.

Library of Congress Cataloging-in-Publication Data
Martino, Alfred C.
Over the end line / by Alfred C. Martino.
p. cm.
Summary: After scoring the winning goal in the county soccer championship,
New Jersey high school senior Jonny finally attains the popularity enjoyed by his
best friend Kyle, until a devastating event changes everything.
ISBN 978-0-15-206121-0
[1. Soccer—Fiction. 2. Friendship—Fiction. 3. Popularity—Fiction. 4. Short Hills (N.J.)—Fiction.] I.
Title.
PZ7.M3674Ov 2009
[Fic]--dc22   2008046464

Manufactured in the United States of America
QUM 10 9 8 7 6 5 4 3 2 1

For Daisy and Sara

Over the End Line

Sunday, November 2

It's morning.

I'm awake. I wish I wasn't.

After a night drowning in alcohol, I'm worse than hung-over—I'm still wasted. So I lie on my bed, staring at the ceiling, my head quivering when my eyes are open. But when they're shut it's as if my bedroom is spinning clockwise and counterclockwise, simultaneously, like one of those amusement rides down the Shore.

My tongue is rough and bone-dry and so swollen it doesn't fit my mouth. I try to swallow. Then try again. But I can't gather any spit, so there's nothing to squeeze down my throat. My arms brace. It's like I can't breathe. *I can't breathe!*

Blackness closes in . . .

I'm gonna pass out . . .

I'm gonna—

In the next moment, air suddenly fills my lungs. I gasp greedily for more until, eventually, my arms go slack. Then the rest of my body, too.

I smell something nasty. I touch my fingers to my face—it's puke—then look down. I'm still wearing my shirt from last night. It's stained. My pillow, too.

The horrid taste in my mouth vaguely reminds me of the grilled cheese I ate for dinner, and the beer and Bacardi that followed. But I'm not sure exactly what remembering means, because memories of last night seem like really bad dreams—fading in, fading out, overlapping, sometimes believable, most times not. I pull off my shirt and wipe my face, then push the pillow off my bed.

There's a knock at the door.

"Ma?"

I hear her muffled voice on the other side—at least I think I do. Something about a friend who's upset, waiting downstairs, waiting for me.

"What, Ma?"

No answer.

Maybe what I thought was my mom's voice was just the rush of heat through our house's air vents. Or the wind outside. Or maybe it was my imagination still sloshing in the backwash at the bottom of that final beer bottle

I might've finished, or spilled, or tossed into the woods near South Pond.

I prop myself up.

Lousy idea.

Vomit climbs up my throat again. I fight to swallow it back down. I close my eyes, but that just makes my head swirl, so I open them again, waiting for the room to settle.

□□□□

Time passes.

I don't know how much. It's too much effort to look at the clock on my nightstand. I feel like crap and doubt a shower is going to change that very much. I manage to sit up, then put my feet to the floor and stand.

"Ahhh!"

Pain rifles up my left leg. I fall to my knees and grab my ankle. It's swollen, a sickly black and blue, and hurts like hell. Is it broken? Did I tear a ligament? I try to remember when and what happened, but can't.

In the corner, something catches my eye—my home whites and a soccer ball. I scored yesterday in the county championship game, right? I scored the game-winner, didn't I? The specifics of how I received the ball and the shot I took are a bit muddled. It was so unlikely, so remarkably unexpected.

I limp over to the window, hold open the curtains, and lean my hands on the sill. It's a raw, blustery morning. No one's on our front lawn, and I don't see anyone outside the Saint-Claires' house across the street.

Then I hear something behind me.

I turn around, hold my breath, and listen.

Sounds like whimpers.

A girl's.

My eyes dart around the room. In the closet. Behind the desk and dresser. Under my bed.

But I see nothing.

The whimpers grow louder. As they do, it becomes apparent to me that something more significant than a soccer game occurred in the past twenty-four hours. On the floor, my jeans and sweatshirt are strewn about. They seem damp and smeared with dirt. A smell of pine and stale beer lingers. So does a sickening feeling. Last night begins to piece itself together.

Walking with Kyle along the dirt path around South Pond . . .

Going to the *circle* . . .

Laughing and joking with guys on the soccer team . . .

Drinking . . .

Hanging out with people in the *crowd* . . .

Drinking a boatload more . . .

Talking to Sloan Ruehl for a while—Sloan Ruehl

for God's sake—the hottest, bitchiest girl at Millburn High . . .

Taking a piss in the woods . . .

Lying face-down on the ground . . .

What happened after?

Did I pass out? Or fall? Or was it something else? And how the hell did I get home?

The whimpers, pained and desperate, crawl across the floor, climb up my body, and burrow inside my mind. I can't stop them. Can't quiet them. I fall back against the wall and slide down. I put my hands over my ears, but the whimpers scratch my eardrums, punishing me.

◻◻◻◻

The bedroom is silent.

My eyes are dry and a searing headache has pierced my temples. Twice more I've booted whatever was left in my stomach into a wastebasket. I wipe my mouth. I'm dizzy. It's late morning, but my room is still dark, and all I want to do is sleep for a long, long time.

Previous August

GIVE-AND-GO, Jonny!"

Kyle and I sprinted down the soccer field at Christ Church, our cleats kicking up flecks of cut grass. He kicked the ball on a diagonal in front of me. I received the pass and knocked it back to him. Kyle ran onto the ball, pushing it far enough ahead to match his long strides; then he offered me another perfect delivery.

The morning sun was harsh as we charged through swarms of gnats and trampled away the last of the dew-slick grass. Kyle crossed the end line, put his cleat on top of the ball to bring it to a stop, then pivoted and started in the opposite direction. I also hit the chalk, turned, and ran upfield.

Kyle was a few steps ahead of me. I tried to close the gap but found myself thinking more about the ache of my thighs and calves than the touch on my passes.

Concentrate . . . concentrate . . . I told myself.

And for a few more runs, from end line to end line, that worked. Eventually though, my legs started to falter.

On our final sprint, Kyle kicked the ball to the side.

"Laps," he said.

I followed him along the outside of the field. His red Manchester United jersey—honoring the great English midfielder Bobby Charlton—gleamed in the sun. Kyle never stepped on a line or cut a corner. That, he would've said, was cheating. I could rattle off the Millburn High School records he crushed, or the Suburban Conference and Essex County records he eclipsed, or the number of goals and assists he compiled to secure all-state selections as a sophomore and junior.

But those were just numbers. You had to see Kyle play with your own eyes. He was magical with a soccer ball, dribbling with the precision of a video game—never so far ahead that an opponent could steal the ball, but never so close that he might have to break stride. And like Charlton, Kyle had a cannon for a shot. Top spin, knuckleball, banana curve—it was as if his shots had eyes for the back of the net.

For Kyle, every season was soccer season. In the winter, he played in a six-on-six indoor league; in the spring, he trained with players on the Rutgers University team. After the school year ended in June, Kyle could have dominated any of the local traveling teams; instead, his father signed us up for a men's league in Hudson County. He thought it would be best. (For me, too, I guess.) It was one of two good things Mr. Saint-Claire did for me—that, and not playing the "surrogate father" crap.

So on Saturday afternoons Kyle and I drove to a hellhole of a neighborhood in Jersey City to play on a perfectly manicured field in the shadow of the New Jersey Turnpike. It was a place where they took their *fútbol* seriously. While I spent most of the time watching from the bench, Kyle took a beating playing against, and with, Cubans and Puerto Ricans just waiting to knock the white out of some rich kid from suburbia.

Our first game typified the season. Opponents kicked at Kyle's shins, made slide tackles from behind, elbowed him for loose balls, while the referees swallowed their whistles and our teammates—if you can call them that— looked on. With a few minutes left, our starting winger pulled a hamstring, so I subbed in. A pass came in my direction. The fullback covering me slipped. I faked a move inside, but pushed the ball toward the end line. Before the ball went out of bounds, I blindly lofted a cross to the goal mouth. Kyle came out of nowhere to jump between two defenders and head the ball past the goalkeeper. A split second later, he was leveled by a third defender.

Kyle got to his feet and shook it off, but I could tell he was hurting. I ran over to him. "Nice job," I said.

He spit grass from his mouth. "Thanks," he replied, and stared at the player who had nailed him. But the guy just kept smirking and the referee, as expected, didn't bother pulling out a yellow card.

By the end of the game, Kyle was bruised and bloodied, but he grabbed his equipment bag and walked, head high, knowing every one of those bastards would be talking about *his* goals when they gathered around their cement lawns and cracked front stoops later that day.

□□□□

I made it a few more laps around the field, but after hours of dribbling, shooting, and passing, my body was finished. I bent over, sucking in deep breaths.

Kyle called out, "We're not done!"

But I waved him off.

As Kyle crossed the far end of the field, I stood in the shade of an oak tree and whisked sweat from my arms and legs with my hands, spraying a mist into the air. I gulped down some water, vaguely noticing the occasional car that passed by on Highland Avenue.

Around me, two bicycles and a half-dozen soccer balls were scattered about. Kyle insisted we ride bikes to and from our training sessions. I think it was a reminder that he wasn't too far removed from the years when he had been just one kid out of many dozens, ordinary in talent, struggling to find a place on a Pee Wee soccer field.

A car horn blared.

I turned.

A white Corvette raced along Highland. Erik Maako was behind the wheel. With freaky eyes, a permanent scowl, and a red-haired goatee, Maako looked, and acted, like a menace (especially with the girls at school). His square shoulders angled down to a thin waist that sat on top of muscular thighs. He was a force on the soccer field, physically imposing on defense, yet creative with the ball when he wanted to be. Last season, as just a sophomore, Maako anchored Millburn's "diamond" defense playing sweeper. This year he would do the same.

Maako looked at me and grinned, pretending to scratch his cheek but conspicuously giving me the finger. I wanted to tell him to drop dead, or flip him off, but his Corvette was already around the bend, and something about doing either of those things near a church didn't seem particularly pious.

Kyle turned up the sideline. "Who was that?"

"Two hints," I said. "One—he's an asshole. Two—Millburn's biggest."

"Screw Maako," Kyle said. "He better've trained hard this summer." Then Kyle raised his eyebrows. "Too bad it wasn't a few incoming sophomore girls, fresh from the junior high."

"Would've been nice," I said, just for the hell of it.

"Soon enough, Jonny, we'll have the pick of the litter."

Senior guys hooking up with sophomore girls—it was practically a rite of passage at Millburn. For the girls, it was an opportunity, early in high school, to cement a reputation for being cool and popular. For the senior guys, it was the long-awaited reward for enduring sophomore and junior year.

Kyle pumped his fist. "It's gonna be a good year . . ." As he continued to jog down the end line, I thought I heard him finish with, "for us."

Some time later, Kyle finally stopped. In spite of the oppressive heat, he looked no worse than if we had shot a casual game of HORSE in his driveway.

"Done?" I said, sitting against a tree.

A hint of a grin emerged on his face. "Done."

SUMMER WAS FADING.

It was the time of year I dreaded most. The days were shorter and at night I could feel a hint of autumn coolness. The grass had changed its scent—it smelled sweet, like shucked corn—but it was more than that. Something stirred in my gut. Maybe it was that the first varsity soccer practice was next Tuesday. Or that the beginning of the school year was just a week after that.

I sprawled out on the couch, half sleeping, half watching television, knowing there wasn't much else to do except rest for tomorrow's training.

My mom was in the kitchen. "Hungry?" she asked.

I looked over at her. "I'm fine."

She went back to tending the potted plants on the windowsill: Boston fern, aloe, ficus, agave, solanum, and her alocasia. She tugged at yellowing leaves, tapped the soils with her fingertips, and sprayed each green canopy with mists of water. In her other hand was a glass of red wine. A half-empty bottle sat on the countertop.

My mom's a hard woman. A survivor, she'd say. *A survivor of what?* I've wondered, but I don't know the answer. She had her day, I'm sure, though she doesn't seem to have many friends now. She talks to Mrs. Saint-Claire from time to time, and once a month some man or another shows up at our front door to take her to dinner, stinking of cologne and trying way too hard to talk to me. Mostly though, my mom goes to work at a bank in Chatham, and reads novels, and takes care of our house well enough. It's just the two of us, so we try to get along. And we pretty much do.

What's there to fight about anyway? Bad things never happen in Short Hills. That's what people have said for as long as the town's been this exclusive community in northern Jersey populated with individuals driven to accumulate, then spawn offspring, educated and ambitious. Who are these people? A blend of nouveau riche with just enough "old money" to preserve the town's status.

Think wealth and privilege don't make a difference? Don't fool yourself. Rich-bitch parents like to plaster the rear windows of their Porsches and Mercedes with stickers from MIT, Amherst, Stanford, and the Ivies. Millburn High is a direct beneficiary of the town's wealth. Sky-high taxes build the best facilities, purchase cutting-edge materials, hire teachers with master's degrees and Ph.D.s, and recruit guidance counselors who are on a first-name basis with admissions directors at the most competitive colleges.

Top of the food chain.

Don't think this is idle, self-important bullshit so I can feel better about myself. Sure, I'm a product of this environment, but I don't give a damn about pedigree. Besides, in this town my mom and I are the ones looking up the money tree. Anyway, in eight months I'll be done with Millburn High. Right after graduation I'll bolt from Short Hills. When I do, I won't come back.

I stretched out my legs, hardly noticing that the cuts on my shins had tightened and semiscabbed. None deserved much more attention than a cursory look anyway. By tomorrow morning, they'd just open up again. I eased back into the cushions, closed my eyes, and tried to drift away. I didn't know where. Just away. Away from the day's heat. Away from my sore and tired body.

Instead, Kyle's voice echoed in my head. "It's gonna be a good year for us . . ."

Was he joking? How could he even hint at something as ridiculous as his senior year and my senior year being similar? Maybe, if everything fell into place for me, I'd sub in for fifteen minutes or so a game this season. Kyle, of course, would enjoy another year of being Millburn's superstar athlete. I'm not sure what he was thinking, but I was damn sure his senior year and my senior year would be worlds apart.

"A good year . . ." I muttered.

I'd never had a good year. I prayed I would when I got to college. Then I'd get respect, covering the sports teams for the school newspaper or working in the athletic department. And after I graduated, I'd be hired by *Sports Illustrated* or the Yankees or maybe even ESPN. Then every year would be a damn good year. Right now, I was just in the wrong town, the wrong high school.

I sometimes imagined what it would be like to live in another town and play on its high school soccer team, with someone other than Pennyweather as coach and Kyle as the resident soccer star. Then I'd get my rightful playing time. And with more playing time I'd score eight, nine, maybe even ten or eleven goals a season. Then it'd be a good year. And when I was really thinking crazy, I wondered if at another school *I* could be the Kyle Saint-Claire of the upcoming senior class, while some other guy would be its Jonathan Fehey. Short of that, could I at least be on equal footing with the others, or—as was my reality at Millburn—would I be a casualty of an omnipotent ranking system beyond my control?

Jacob's Ladder.

That's what it's called.

The rumor is that someone thought the wretched lost souls of our class should be "given their due." So, at the end of our sophomore year, a ladder was drawn on a sheet of paper. The wretched lost souls were hung from the lowest rungs; those in the crowd from the highest rungs; the rest of our class, somewhere in between. The hierarchy had been there all along. Now it had been made real. At least on paper.

They said the original and only copy of the ladder was hidden in the stacks on the second floor of the town library, neatly folded inside a book so obscure it would never be borrowed. But it's all a mystery. Or a myth. It's kind of like the Bible in that way. I mean, does anyone really know who wrote the Bible? Yet millions live by its words, if only to pass judgment on others. The same was true with the ladder. The creator intended to be anonymous, and through that anonymity, gave the ladder authority.

But these vagaries don't imply that the ladder's existence is in question. It's not. It's tangible, even if it can't be held and examined. It's the material from which our class's social fabric is woven, securing the fate of each of us. And don't mistake my frustration for resignation. A thousand times I've thought, *I'm better than that.* In fact, every day of my junior year, I walked the crowded hallways and sat in the classrooms, praying that something, somehow, might change—hoping against hope that I might be moving up a rung or two, that someone in the crowd might recognize that I'm more than where the ladder—

Glass shattered.

"Damn it," I heard my mom say.

"You all right?"

She let out a long sigh. "Just being clumsy."

"Need help?"

"I'm fine."

Holding on to the countertop, my mom picked up the glass pieces, then tore off a handful of paper towels to soak up the wine. She had a slightly bothered look on her face. From more than just spilled wine. Was she thinking about my dad? A strange thought, but the first that came to mind. I think about him sometimes. I don't remember much, though. I only knew him for a short time, when I was a little kid, before he left us. I suppose I should be thankful for any time I had with him. I've kept some of his stuff. Rather, I've taken things that my mom stored away in the attic or hid in the secret drawer of her vanity. A watch with his initials and the date 3-5-1974 engraved on the back. A light blue button-down shirt he wore to work. Ticket stubs from a Cosmos–Rowdies NASL game he took me to.

Thinking about my dad is like opening my eyes in the middle of the night and not being able to distinguish dreams from reality. So I try to fit these vague memories together, like puzzle pieces, with the hope of seeing some kind of truth. A bigger picture. But that's never really worked.

I wondered how often my mom thought about him. She's never said anything, except once when we were driving down the parkway to my aunt's house for a holiday dinner. She told me her life with him, for a time, was nice. *Nice.* That was it, nothing more. I always thought she said it just to appease me, because when I looked at her eyes, I saw something that she never revealed in words. Pain.

I've asked questions like, What does "nice" mean? Was it ever better than that? Why isn't he here? But no one is around to hear me, and so the questions remain lost in the silence between my mom and me, and I go back to being an only child of a single mom in this rich town, much of the time feeling way out of place. I think she knows I feel like this—my mom kind of reads me really well. Who knows? Maybe she feels the same way.

My mom finished cleaning the floor. She walked in from the kitchen and leaned against the doorway. She had another glass of wine in her hand.

"Should I leave the outside lights on?" she asked.

"No."

"Not going out?"

I shook my head.

"Where's Kyle?"

"Don't know."

I could've told her Kyle was partying at the circle, but she wouldn't have known what or where the circle was, and then I'd have to explain it all. Then she wouldn't have understood why I wasn't there, too, and I'd have to explain that as well. It's just easier to let her think her son is this really happy kid who's friends with all the popular people at school.

"Everything okay?" she asked.

"Yeah."

"You sure?"

"Yeah."

"I don't know . . ." she said. It seemed she was trying to get at something. "The two of you have been friends a long time."

"Ma, I'm fine. Kyle's fine. We're all fine." I sank down in the couch and stared at the television.

Kyle and I had been close since the day the Saint-Claires moved in across the street. As kids, we played capture-the-flag until midnight in the summer. Often I stayed at the Saint-Claires' shore house in Brielle. We built snow forts in the winter and played ice hockey on North Pond when the flag was up. Kyle would sleep over at my house and I'd sleep over at his. We grew up catching lightning bugs, colds, Yankee–Red Sox games, and a fist fight or two. Or three. We were best friends, and best friendships endured anything. At least I thought.

Then things changed. I don't think my mom had a

clue about that. Kyle and I trained together for the up-coming varsity season and, when school started, I'd get a ride from him on most mornings. But that was it. The truth was, ever since seventh grade, we lived different lives at Millburn. I sometimes wondered what would've happened to me if I'd never quit baseball to concentrate on soccer. I was going to be a soccer star, I'd convinced myself. But it never happened, and that decision was now long in the past.

"My son," my mom said, with a thoughtful smile, "a se-nior in high school."

I frowned. "It's no big deal."

"You'll be the talk of the school."

"Not likely."

People at Millburn saw only what they wanted to see. If they wanted to think you were cool, then you were cool. Or smart. Or an athlete. Or hot. If they wanted to think you were a nobody, then you were that, regardless of how you saw yourself. Some thought my friendship with Kyle was a fraud, that he had taken pity on me. Others believed I had dirt on Kyle and that he only main-tained the façade of a friendship in return for my silence. But no one knew the real me. No one could get inside my head. Of course, that didn't matter. What the people in my class thought of me was my reality. And, in the end, my reality was that I couldn't go with Kyle to the circle to hang out with the crowd—people I've lived in the same town with all my life—because of the ladder. Sure, I was about to be a senior. Sure, I should've felt something special. But I didn't.

"It'll be the time of your life," my mom said, as if she were imparting wisdom for the ages.

"And you know this how?" I said.

She shook her head. "You don't think I was a high school senior once?"

"Way back when," I said with a grin.

"It wasn't *that* long ago, mister," she said. "High school is high school. Senior years are special. You'll see what I mean."

I rolled my eyes. "Whatever."

The Tuesday after Labor Day, the sun would come up, I'd dress, get a ride, then walk in the Millburn High main entrance as I had hundreds of times as a sophomore and junior, as I had as a seventh-, eighth-, and ninth-grader at the junior high. Senior year would be just another in a long chain of endless years of academic endurance. There'd be different teachers, different classrooms, different books, but it'd all be the same. Barring a miracle on the soccer field, nothing would make it especially memorable.

My mom frowned and shook her head. "With an attitude like that . . ."

I had nothing else to say. I waited for her last words that in any of our discussions were the closing credits, the pithy epilogue. She walked back into the kitchen. I heard her shoes click on the tiled floor, then stop.

"You never know how things'll turn out," she said. "They just might surprise you. But you have to at least *try* to enjoy yourself."

That was it? I didn't expect her to have the definitive answer on how I was going to make it through the year without crashing and burning, but I certainly expected something more, something a bit more tangible.

I looked back toward the kitchen and heard the spray bottle.

Then heard it again.

IT HAD BEEN AN ESPECIALLY humid morning. I was wiped out; Kyle was, too. In the middle of the Christ Church field, he took ten paces in one direction, then another ten perpendicular to that. We used our shirts, water bottles, and whatever else we could find to mark the boundaries. Kyle brushed the sweat from his forehead and stood on one edge of the square, the soccer ball at his feet. I stood on the opposite edge, facing him.

"Ready?" Kyle said. "You first."

He flicked the ball to me.

I caught it with my instep and brought it down to the ground. Kyle charged at me. I shielded him with my body. My cleats danced on and around the ball, pushing it forward, drawing it back, nudging it left, then right. I imagined myself a player much greater, and I saw the two of us battling on a field infinitely grander—like Wembley or Estadio Azteca. Kyle was with me every step, trying to knock me off balance with his shoulders and hips. Still, the ball remained in my control.

"Not bad, Jonny," Kyle said.

Sometimes he could be so damn patronizing.

"I'll let ya touch the ball when I'm done," I said. Kyle pushed into me, but I held my ground. "Shoulda eaten your Wheaties, Saint-Claire."

That was all Kyle was going to take. He stepped on my cleat, then elbowed past me to steal the ball.

"So that's how we're playin'?" I said.

He gave me a wry smile. "Get used to it."

I bent down, tied my laces, then stood again. It was his turn. I charged at Kyle, leaning my body against his, darting my cleats at the ball. To his surprise (and mine), I quickly made the steal.

"Gee, that wasn't *too* easy," I said.

"A stroke of luck, wiseass," Kyle said.

We took turns, playing keep-away for another half hour. It had been a good training session for me. Great, really. My passes had been crisp, my shots on target, and earlier, when the two of us ran laps, the end lines and sidelines seemed shorter than usual.

"Last one," Kyle said.

I moved toward him. He stepped over the ball, faked one way, then pulled it backwards. I closed the distance between the two of us, then bumped him. He held me off. I bumped him again, feeling the intensity in his body— he was *not* going to give up the ball. But I pushed forward, trapping him in a corner.

I lunged at Kyle, shooting my leg between his, my cleat catching his shin. Kyle stood strong, controlling the ball with one foot. But I was relentless. I knocked him off balance; he recovered. I pressed further. For a moment, as the ball moved close to the edge of the square, Kyle seemed frustrated. I relished the thought and moved in for the—

Bang!

I was on the ground looking up. "What was that?" I said, wiping my lip where his elbow had hit me.

"An accident."

"An accident?"

"Yeah."

"Bull."

Kyle stood above me. "You wanna play with the big boys? You gotta get tougher."

"You just don't like me beating you."

"Never happened," he said. "So I wouldn't know."

"Did today."

"Jonny," Kyle said, scooping the ball off the ground with his cleat, then juggling it with his knees to his head, "you're dreamin'."

"No, I think I pissed off the mighty Saint-Claire." I stood up and grabbed my shirt. "I did, didn't I?"

I got on my bike. Kyle got on his.

"That was garbage," I said. "And you know it."

□□□□

With the noon sun above us and the black steel trusses of Redemption Bridge ahead, Kyle and I pedaled up Lake Road. My thighs were jellied, my shins bruised, and heat rising from the pavement had me sweating bullets. Kyle pulled a water bottle from his backpack, took a gulp, then swung his bike beside mine and passed the bottle. I took a swig and handed it back.

"What're you smirking about?" he asked. "Thought you were good today, is that it?"

"I was feelin' it."

Kyle shook his head, dismissively.

That pissed me off. "Know what, Kyle? I was goddamn great today. You know it, and I know it." I tilted my face into the sun. "Now, excuse me while I bask in my magnificence."

"Heat's fried your brain."

"Not as bad as I burned your ass in keep-away."

"Think so?"

"Know so."

"How about you do it in front of Pennyweather next week," Kyle said. "Better yet, do it in a game this season. Then we'll talk."

I shot a look at him. "What's your problem?"

"How important is soccer to you?" he asked.

"What're you, my mom?"

"So you like riding the bench?" Kyle pushed.

"Best seat in town," I quipped.

We continued up Lake Road in silence and, for a while, I thought we'd make it all the way home without saying another word. But then Kyle suddenly cut in front of me and slammed on his brakes. I stopped short. He grabbed my handlebars.

"You want more playing time?"

I rolled my eyes. "Gee, ya think?"

"I'm serious. You want more playing time, don't ya?"

"I played last year," I said. "Averaged nine minutes a game. Nine minutes and fifteen seconds, to be exact."

Kyle shook his head. "Was that enough?"

"Maybe."

"Was it?"

"No," I conceded.

"The starting lineup should be your goal," he said. "If not, you're wasting your time."

I looked at him. "You really think I've been draggin' my ass around Christ Church field with you so I can spend the next two and a half months planted on the bench?" I backed my bike up until he let go, then I started up Lake Road again. "I got everything under control."

But the truth was other people had more control over what happened to me than I did. Whether it was some anonymous jerk creating the ladder, or Pennyweather deciding if and when I played. On and off the field, in and out of school, other people controlled so much of what I could or couldn't do. I hated it, but had to live with it.

Kyle was behind me. "Things are gonna be different this year."

"Different?" I said. "How?"

"It's senior year."

"So?"

"Time to live it up. Take advantage of everything. Like sophomore girls. But you know what'll be the coolest?"

"What?"

Kyle caught up to me. "No rules," he said.

"No rules?"

"Yeah."

"What 'no rules'?"

"No *rules*."

"Kyle, you already don't have rules. You do what you want, when you want, how you want."

His face turned hard. "You think I can do whatever I want?"

"It's not what I think," I said. "It's what I know."

"Jonny, everyone watches me. All the time. Everything I do." It must have looked as though I thought he was full of it, because Kyle went on as if he had to convince me. "Remember our second game against Caldwell last year, on their field? We won, one to nothing. Clinched the conference title."

I remembered. I had played most of the second quarter. I had four touches on the ball, took a shot that went wide of the net, and even made a defensive stop on a Caldwell give-and-go in our zone.

But this wasn't about me; it was about Kyle. He dominated both ends of the field, controlling the midfield play with punishing tackles and initiating a half-dozen offensive attacks that led to scoring chances. Each time he touched the ball, Caldwell players knocked him down or slid into him with their cleats up. A few dozen fouls were called and the referees handed out three yellow cards. Blood streaked Kyle's calves, but he never stopped running, never showed any quit. On Millburn's lone goal, with just six minutes left, Kyle weaved his way through three Caldwell defenders, then set up Tony Gallo with an easy tap-in. Kyle's play that afternoon was, in a word, incredible.

"There was a problem," Kyle said.

"A problem?"

"Yeah."

"What?"

"All I got was that assist," he said. "Forget that I owned the midfield. Forget that my assist set up the winning goal and all that Gallo had to do was stand there like a statue and let the ball hit him. Forget that I cleared two Caldwell corner kicks from our goal area."

"You were good," I said.

"Better than good, Jonny," Kyle said. "I was awesome."

I rolled my eyes, even though I knew he was right.

"Know the first thing I heard when we came off the field?" Kyle said.

I didn't.

"Was something wrong with me?" Kyle half laughed. "After all, something *had* to be wrong with Kyle Saint-Claire if he hadn't scored. I even heard someone's dad say it didn't seem as if my head was in the game. The *Item* wrote that I had an 'uncharacteristically quiet game.' Can you believe that? Jonny, I can't do anything I want. I can't do anything at all without people in this town examining every little detail."

"At least they notice."

"I don't want it."

"Attention comes with the territory," I said. "The soccer star gets nearly all of it. Other starters get some. Those of us riding the bench, waiting for Pennyweather to dole out a few minutes of playing time, get nothing. Zip. Zilch. Nada."

"You gotta change that," Kyle said.

"I wish," I said. "But it's not gonna happen."

"Why not?"

"Not at Millburn. The last day of school next June, the bell rings and I step out. That's when it changes, Kyle. That's the big equalizer. Until then, the way it is, is the way it is."

We weren't far from Redemption Bridge. When we got closer, I stepped off my bike and picked up a quarter-sized rock.

"Is the mighty Saint-Claire ready to tempt Fate?" I said.

Mounted on one of the bridge's railings was a weathered metal plaque. It read:

In June of 1780, valiant residents of what would later be named Short Hills, under the leadership of Gen. Nathanael Greene, helped repel British and Hessian troops in the Battle of Springfield, thus protecting Gen. George Washington's head-quarters in Morristown. This battle marked the final British incursion into New Jersey.

Over the decades, the plaque had become a kind of good-luck target. After a big soccer or football victory, Millburn players would drive over the bridge and throw bottles at the plaque, raining down broken glass into the creek below. Every year, on the last day of school, seniors would douse the plaque in paint and brush across epithets such as "Scummit Sucks," a pleasantry for our cross-town rival, Summit. The town's public works department would quickly have the plaque repainted black, but hundreds of dents remained.

I held up the stone for Kyle to see. "Since you hate all the attention, how 'bout this? I hit the plaque and you don't get to be with *any* sophomore girls until soccer season ends. I don't care how much they're begging for you. Got it?"

"Jonny . . ."

I took aim, reached my arm back, and threw. The stone sailed through the air, began to dip, then hit dead center.

"The plaque has spoken!" I shouted.

Maybe I was still jacked up from the training session, or maybe the flight of the rock gave me the small victory over Kyle that I needed, but I momentarily lost my head. Without thinking, I climbed up on the top railing, putting my hand on one of the truss's diagonal supports. The railing wobbled. For a frightening instant, I was staring down at a rusted metal ladder that led to a repair platform below me, and immense rocks jutting from the withered creek below that. My stomach dropped. *Oh, shit.* I almost fell. Thankfully, I gained my composure and quickly stepped down from the railing.

"Jonny?" Kyle said.

Before I turned to answer him, I heard voices. I looked below. Sitting against the bridge's abutment were Kyle's younger sister, Stephanie, her friend, Trinity, and a girl whom I didn't know. In front of them, five candles burned.

Animated and pretentious, Trinity wore a black lace shirt and pants, black boots, and maroon lipstick, with a Celtic knot around her neck. There was a streak of red in her otherwise jet-black hair. A cigarette in one hand and a lighter in the other, she held court, spouting more of that self-important garbage that surely wouldn't fly when they got to high school. "We're the lone bastions of individuality in a town of elitists and conformists," she said to the other two girls. "We have to watch out for each other. All the time."

Stephanie raised her eyes. Trinity spun around and shouted, "What're you fuckin' spying on us?"

"You kiss your mom with that mouth?" I said.

Trinity laughed. "Jonny-boy, I'm not the one who has to worry about rumors about kissing my mother."

"Whatever you say, *Beverly.*"

She shot me the finger. "Screw you, Jonny, you know that's not my name!"

I couldn't help but laugh. Choosing the pseudo-religious Trinity as her adopted name was stupid. Claiming that Trinity was a tribute to her Celtic ancestors, when

everyone at Millburn knew her parents were major bene-
factors at Temple B'nai Jeshurun, was ridiculously stupid.

Stephanie yelled up to me, "Hey, tell my brother he's
driving us to the Livingston Mall later."

Then the three girls huddled together and started gig-
gling. I stepped away from the railing. I wasn't surprised
they were there. Stephanie knew our neighborhood as
well as any of us. When we were young and Kyle let her
play kick-the-can, she hardly ever got caught because she
had figured out the best hiding places. I'd seen her before
at North Pond, writing in a journal or reciting from a book.
Now, I guess, her spot was the creek beneath Redemption
Bridge.

I gestured to Kyle. "You're driving your sister to
the mall."

"Jonny, I didn't agree to it."

"Hey, she's your sister. You two work it out."

"No, the bet," he said. "I never agreed to the bet."

I shook my head. "That's weak."

"Jonny, with an arm like yours," Kyle said, sarcasti-
cally, "I *knew* you'd hit the plaque."

I reached down to pick up another rock, but then
thought better of it. I might miss the plaque and hit one of
the girls down below, which, even if it had been Trinity,
wouldn't have been worth the headache afterward. So I
picked up my bike instead, and Kyle and I pedaled across
the bridge.

"How 'bout this?" I said as we continued up Lake Road. "Three tosses from the dock. Longest throw wins, same as always. We'll put this whole sophomore girls thing to rest."

"And when I win?" Kyle said.

"In the unlikely event you win, then they're off-limits to me during the season." But that didn't seem like nearly enough, so I added, "For my *entire* senior year."

Kyle hesitated, then nodded his approval.

"When are we gonna do this?" I asked.

"Tomorrow afternoon. After we're done training," Kyle said. "You got until then to sweat it."

I STOOD AT THE SQUAT RACK, preparing for another set, when I heard my mom's footsteps coming down the basement stairs. I looked over. She was wearing jewelry and her nicest clothes, and she had obviously been to the beauty salon.

"I'll be out tonight," she said.

She seemed to be expecting a question from me. But I had none.

"Will you come up and say hello?" she said. "That would be the respectful thing to do."

"Ma, you see me working out."

She pursed her lips, but I knew she understood. I had nothing to say to these men. They usually asked me about where I wanted to go to college, or what my major would be, or whether I was a Mets or Yankees fan. I hated the questions. I knew none of her dates cared what my answers were anyway.

"I wrote down the phone number of the restaurant," she said. "It's on the kitchen counter. There are leftovers in the refrigerator. You'll be all right?"

"I've been alone before," I said.

"I just want you to know where we'll be. So, how do I look?"

"Nice."

I waited until I heard the front door close. It was me alone in the basement, me alone in the house. I didn't have to be down here killing myself. I could've been sitting my ass on the sofa. No one would've known either way. I gripped the barbell with both hands and ducked my head underneath, pressing my upper back and shoulders against the steel. In the mirror on the wall, I stared at my reflection. My face was flushed, and sweat darkened the collar and armpits of my shirt—the céleste and white striped jersey of the greatest striker of all time, the player Argentina and the world called el Matador.

Mario Kempes.

Jugador de fútbol.

El número diez.

I breathed in and out, forcefully and loudly. Maybe, as a kid in Córdoba, Kempes spent nights alone in his basement lifting weights and dreaming of soccer glory. Maybe he had doubts, like I did. Maybe he wondered if it'd all be worth it someday, like I did.

My body flexed as I straightened up, lifting the bar off the rack. The plates jostled and clanked. I took two choppy steps backwards and raised my eyes toward the ceiling. Down. My hips lowered until my thighs were parallel to the floor. Then I exploded up, and was standing.

"One."

Quick breath. And down again.

So what if I was a returning varsity-letter winner? That meant nothing. I played only when a starting winger or striker needed a break. Or at the end of a blowout. Up! Slowly . . .

"Two."

Quick breath. Quick breath. Down.

Scored one goal, had one assist last season. Numbers that suck. Rode the bench too damn much. Up! Struggling . . . struggling . . .

"Three."

Quick breath. Quick breath. Quick breath. Quick breath. Deep breath. Down.

Too bad Pennyweather couldn't see me now. I'll be better this season. Much better. Up!

I pressed my feet into the floor, lifting with my shoulders, arms, and upper back. My thighs quivered. They were quitting.

"Not yet," I grunted.

The bar tilted, but I recovered. Finally, I was upright. I shuffled forward and crashed the bar back onto the rack.

"Four . . ."

My head hung. I was hardly in control of my breaths. I looked down. The gash above my knee had opened. Screw it. Screw Pennyweather, for that matter. Probably figures it'd be a waste having a senior like me taking up minutes that could be given to a sophomore or junior touted as a future soccer star. Can't pass on the next Kyle Saint-Claire, right? God forbid.

I sat down on the bench and closed my eyes. My heart pounded. Sweat trickled down my forehead. I wiped it away with the sleeve of my jersey. I expected the season's first practice to be brutal. Running laps, endless cals, monotonous drills. But the toughest part would be the competition. Fighting to make the varsity squad. Fighting for playing time. Fighting for a starting position. It would be that way every practice.

Still, most of it was out of my hands. Pennyweather chose who made the varsity team, who started, who played, and for how many minutes. He remained Millburn's soccer czar, answering to no one, with the authority to make unilateral decisions. At least, that's the way it seemed.

Rumors told a different story.

Four years ago, a few parents whose soccer-playing sons would benefit the most in upcoming years had their say about who would fill the varsity head coaching vacancy. Under the guise of the newly formed Youth Soccer Association of Millburn–Short Hills, they "recommended" to the town's board of education that Pennyweather be hired onto the high school's computer science staff and, of course, as soccer coach. Did cash pass hands? Were favors promised? Who knows. But the names of other candidates were quickly dropped from consideration, and Pennyweather, who had been a middle school coach at nearby Union, ascended to Millburn's soccer throne. Everyone got what they wanted.

I looked at myself in the mirror, again. I wondered if Kempes had to deal with garbage like this when he played on his first club team, Instituto Atlético Central Córdoba.

I stepped to the squat rack, pulled the plates off the bar, and set them against the wall. My thighs were shot, but it felt good. All this would make me a half step faster, I was sure. If not immediately, then by the first varsity practice. Or the first game on the schedule. If not then, then certainly at some point this season.

I moved the barbell from the squat rack down to the bench, and slid the plates back on. Had to work on my arms. My throwing arm, especially. I was going to beat Kyle tomorrow. I sat on the bench, rolled up my sleeves, then lay back and set my hands shoulder-width apart on the bar.

I breathed in.

And lifted.

WITH NORTH POND ON OUR left and Redemption Bridge ahead in the distance, Kyle and I cut off Lake Road into the woods that surrounded South Pond. Walking through overgrown brush and around large trees, we made our way onto the dirt path that hugged the shoreline, stepping over exposed roots and kicking through discarded fishing line that got caught on our sneakers. The stink of algae filled the air, and sunlight glimmered off the green lily pads that dotted the murky surface.

Throwing stones from the dock was our way of settling arguments. The first time was when Kyle and I were kids fighting over who was a better catcher: Yankee great Thurman Munson or the Red Sox's pompous Carlton Fisk. Kyle made the mistake of saying he was glad Munson went down in that plane crash, and that the autographed baseball on my bedroom dresser wasn't worth the cheap plastic case I had it in.

"I'm gonna beat you to a pulp," I told him.

"You couldn't hurt a fly, faggy Fehey," Kyle said.

"Screw you, Saint-Queer!"

I remember how wide Kyle's eyes were, and I could tell by the anger inside me that mine must've been just as crazed. Kyle ran onto my front lawn and hit me with a punch. I did the same to him, before he tackled me to the grass. We pushed and grabbed each other, cursing and yelling, before finally letting go.

"Get outta here!" I said.

"It's my street," Kyle yelled.

"Yeah?" I said, stepping onto Lake Road. "What're ya gonna do now?"

The fight was noticed by Mr. Saint-Claire at their front door, and my mom at our front door. We were both called inside. I stormed away, swearing so loud, I almost couldn't hear Kyle swearing back at me. I brushed by my mom and bolted upstairs to my bedroom. For an hour or two I fumed.

But eventually my anger subsided. Enough that I grabbed my shortstop's glove and went back outside. I sat on the curb, tossing pebbles into the street gutter. Soon, Stephanie rode down the Saint-Claires' driveway on her bicycle. She turned figure eights and circles in front of me, ringing a silver bell with plastic tassels on her handlebars.

"You in a fight with Kyle?" she asked.

"None of your business," I said.

"My friend Beverly's coming over. She lives only a few streets away. She'll be here soon. We're gonna hide. No one'll find us. Not Kyle, not you, not anyone."

"No one'll wanna find ya."

But Stephanie was oblivious to what I said. Back then, she was just kind of in the background. She wasn't pretty or ugly, but something of a brown-haired, dimpled, any-girl. People mostly knew her as Kyle's little sister, which didn't seem to bother her, tagging along when he and I kicked a soccer ball around or listened to music in his bedroom, content to live in his shadow. She was two grades younger than us, which, at the time, made her seem like just a kid.

Mostly though, I felt bad for Stephanie, so when Kyle wasn't around, I'd fix her bicycle chain, or pump a flat tire, or help her look for her kitten, Ginger, when it got loose. The last time, I found Ginger lying dead along Lake Road near the drainage pipe that connected the two ponds. I wish I hadn't. I was pretty sure our neighbor's Rottweiler, King, got to her. Would've been better for me to put Ginger deep in the pipe and tell Stephanie that she probably ran away. But Stephanie figured out the truth.

A few days later, King got into an open bag of poisonous fertilizer in the Saint-Claires' garage. He was found dead on a nearby lawn, foaming from his mouth. When I saw Stephanie riding her bike down Lake Road, not long after, she seemed almost pleased.

That was the beginning of an uneasy familiarity, if you can call it that, between Stephanie and me. Though we didn't talk to each other very much, we knew enough about each other. I knew how pained she looked when she cried, and how she closed her eyes and kind of snorted when she laughed, and that she buried Ginger in a jewelry box her grandmother had given her for Easter (I dug the hole), hoping she'd forever be protected from worms.

Eventually, Kyle came around from the back of his house, an outfielder's glove on his hand, a hardball in the webbing. He shooed Stephanie away and sat at the curb. A few minutes passed as we both tossed pebbles at the gutter. Then the tosses became challenges. How many times in a row one of us could get a pebble down the sewer grate on a bounce. On two bounces. With our left hands. Over our backs. When we had run out of variations, Kyle called out, "Ten paces." He marched out the steps on his lawn, while I did the same on my lawn. Then I said, "Whip it!"

The ball made a *thwat* sound when it hit my glove. "Weak," I said.

"Just warmin' up," Kyle answered back.

We had played baseball together since the youngest levels of Little League, teammates some years, opponents others. I played shortstop and batted cleanup; Kyle played right field and usually batted last.

"Come on, *really* whip it!" I said. After catching his throw, I shrugged. "That the best ya got?"

"You can rub your hand now," Kyle said.

Back and forth we went, each time trying to throw the baseball harder than the time before. Soon, our fight was in the past. The score, however, was not settled. Tossing pebbles into the sewer was not significant enough, while whipping a baseball required the cooperation of a stationary, and willing, person to catch it. Neither produced a winner. So I came up with the idea of throwing three, and only three, stones from the dock—and the three immutable rules.

First, farthest throw wins. Simple. Significant. Glorious.

Second, the challenger sets the consequences. Always.

Third, a challenge can never be refused without wearing the label of "Wussy for Life" for the next month.

I beat Kyle that first time, and I beat him later that summer. But over time, things changed. Fifth grade turned into sixth grade. I could still throw hard, but Kyle had grown bigger and stronger. Then sixth grade turned into seventh, and our athletic abilities diverged. I denied this for a long time. I mean, what kid wants to admit his best friend has surpassed him athletically?

My mom bought me a bench, a barbell, and free

weights. Then the squat rack. I think she figured they were things Dad would have gotten me had he been around. So I lifted weights and played baseball and soccer. After a couple of years, I hung up my baseball glove because I thought soccer was my sport and that by high school I'd be a varsity star (that turned out to be a mistake). Still, I took every opportunity to challenge Kyle, hoping one day to see the tide turn back in my favor.

◻◻◻◻

"How's your arm?" I said, trying to sound as disingenuous as possible.

"You're gonna find out," Kyle said.

"I'll handle my victory in a gracious and gentlemanly manner," I said. "I certainly won't let any of those incoming sophomore girls know that I whupped you. *Twice* in two days."

"Keep talking, Jonny," Kyle said with an assured smile.

As we continued on the path, a certain irony was not lost on me. We were at South Pond, the arena in which Kyle and I would challenge each other again, and yet past the dock at the opposite end of the pond, behind a wall of pine trees, was the circle. Between the tree branches, I could almost see the street pavement. It seemed so innocuous, and yet that was the cul-de-sac where classmates on the highest rungs of the ladder had parties, smoking pot, getting wasted, and fooling around.

At an open area in front of the dock, marked by an overturned rowboat, Kyle and I rooted around for stones. I found three good ones—each was smooth but not slippery; heavy but light enough to travel a long way. Kyle held up his three.

"I'll give ya last licks," I said.

"You're up then," Kyle said.

When I walked to the end of the dock, it creaked and shook slightly. Across the pond was a large patch of lily pads. But that wasn't far enough. Past the lily pads, a jagged rock jutted from the surface. That wasn't far enough. Beyond the jagged rock was the water's edge. Still, that wasn't far enough. Finally, the water's edge gave way to a muddy shore that climbed sharply into a dirt embankment. *That* was the goal.

I held my breath, stepped back a few planks, and launched the first stone. It was a good throw, but not great. The stone arced past the last lily pad before disappearing into the water.

"Not bad," Kyle said. He seemed pleased with the challenge.

I moved aside, letting him step onto the dock. He wasted little time, tensing for a moment, then with an effortless motion of his arm, let loose a throw. We watched the stone soar beyond the lily pads, the jagged rock, the water's edge, and stop dead in the soft mud.

"You're ahead," I said.

Kyle stepped back, sweeping his arm to give me room.

I took my position on the dock, wondering whether my ego had provoked a challenge my arm couldn't win. I held the second stone, placing my fingertips on its creases. This one felt good. I took a big step and lunged. The stone took off from my outstretched hand and sailed. Farther this time, I could tell immediately. It streaked through the sunlight, well above the lily pads and jagged rock, and disappeared into the mud.

I had hoped for more.

"We'll call it even," Kyle said as we switched positions. He readied himself for a second throw, and then cocked his arm.

"Maako wants to take over midfield this season," I said.

Kyle stopped and looked over his shoulder.

I shrugged. "It's what I heard."

Maybe I heard someone say Maako's name, and maybe I heard someone else say he wanted to take over something. So I extrapolated a little. No doubt, in any other years before or after the Saint-Claire Era, Maako would have been *the* soccer stud at Millburn, beyond reproach even with his obnoxious personality. Instead, with Michael Maynard playing stopper at the top of the diamond, Trevor

Jones at left fullback, and Solomon Smith on the right, Maako carried the burden of being the team's last line of defense against giving up goals, and the unthinkable— losing. For that reason, I would've bet my life that Maako did entertain the thought of taking over center midfield— where the game is controlled—a position that Kyle considered his stage. Alone.

"Nice try," Kyle said with a bemused look. "You should have more confidence in your arm."

"I do."

"Then why the distraction?"

"But I thought the mighty Saint-Claire ignores distractions."

"I do."

"Even about Maako?"

"Especially about Maako."

I would've preferred to ignore Maako, too. But as much as I hated his guts, he couldn't be ignored. Not by me. Not even by Kyle.

And maybe his name did distract Kyle, because the instant the stone left his hand, it was obvious the throw— though a strong one—didn't have enough elevation. Gravity brought the stone earthbound, where it skipped off the jagged rock and rolled up the shoreline to the top of the embankment.

"Bounces don't count," I said.

"Wiseass."

"Just confirming the rules, Kyle. Just confirming the rules."

I saved my best stone for last. I marked my footing to the edge of the dock, and wiped away any concern about throwing out my shoulder. There was too much at stake. I could live with a little pain. This was for glory, and glory was eternal.

And I did hit all the steps I'd measured, reaching my arm back and snapping it through the air, elbow first, forearm next, wrist last, my left sneaker firmly planted on the final plank. The stone rocketed out of my hand on a perfect trajectory. It rose through the air, leveled off, eased back down to earth, and, finally, landed halfway up the embankment.

"*That,* Saint-Claire, is how you do it!" I said. I turned to him and unleashed what was surely the biggest grin in the world.

"You got hold of that one," he said.

"Damn right I did," I said. "You're up. Last throw. Think about what's at stake."

Kyle stepped onto the dock. He had a faraway gaze, as if searching for something in the distance. It gave him a serious look, the kind of look that people in school thought made him seem even more extraordinary. His body stiffened with a focus so intense, it was startling. He didn't study the stone, he didn't take a running start, he didn't edge closer to the end of the dock. He just stared across

South Pond. And stared. And stared some more. Until, it seemed, his mere concentration would draw the opposite shore closer.

"While we're young," I said.

Kyle shot a look toward me. "You see, Jonny," he said, matter-of-factly, "someone's always gunning for me."

He then reared back and launched the stone. *What the*—I couldn't complete the thought. His arm whooshed, I mean *really* whooshed. My eyes and brain scrambled to understand how a stone could travel in that kind of arc, with that kind of distance. It wasn't possible. My God, it just wasn't possible.

But it *was* possible, and it happened and I did see it, so I can never deny the truth without being a full-on liar. The stone climbed high into the air, well above the pond, beginning its descent as it passed over the lily pads, then the shoreline, then the embankment. It disappeared into the woods beyond the embankment, like a shooting star shining in splendor, then slipping into the black of night without a trace.

Kyle slapped his hands free of dirt, raised his eyebrows, and stepped off the dock like it was the easiest, most commonplace thing he had ever done. I followed him, but stared back incredulously at the distance the stone had covered, still wondering if there was, somehow, another explanation.

As we walked back down the path toward Lake Road,

Kyle sniffed the air, then suddenly put his arm out to stop me from walking any farther.

"Smell that?" he said.

"Smell what?"

He sniffed again. "That."

I breathed in, but couldn't smell anything more than the stink of pond water.

"It's here," Kyle said.

"Here?"

"Can you smell it?"

"No," I said.

"I didn't think you could, Jonny," Kyle said, grinning. "That's because it's the sweet smell of sophomore girls."

WITH MY EQUIPMENT BAG in hand, I rumbled down the stairs to the hallway. "Gotta go," I called out to my mom.

"I'm getting dressed," she said from behind her bedroom door. "I'll see you after work. We'll have dinner together."

In the kitchen, I opened the refrigerator and pulled out a bottle of water and an orange. I yawned, then yawned again. And each time I did, my body shivered. I was too anxious to eat much of anything—it might end up on the field. Not that the nervousness was unfamiliar. The start of the season always had me on edge. If I wanted to make my mark on the team, I'd have to prove myself each practice, each step of the way. Starting today.

I heard a car horn.

I looked out the kitchen window. Kyle's black BMW, which his father bought him last year for making first-team all-state, idled on Lake Road. After a final check to make sure I had my shin guards, cup, and athletic tape, I walked through the dining room to get my cleats in the garage.

Instead, they were hanging from the doorknob.

That was a surprise.

I held the cleats up. Cleaned of dirt and grass, the laces were bright white and the leather shined as much as when I first bought them. I looked back toward the stairs to the second floor. Mom and I never talked about soccer, and I certainly didn't think she knew when the season started. Sometimes I wondered if it mattered to her what was going on in my life. Then she'd go and do something like this. I wondered when she took the time. I wondered why.

"Thanks, Ma," I said, quietly.

◻◻◻◻

Underneath the Millburn football field grandstand, Kyle and I entered the crowded locker room. The walls were slick with perspiration and the air smelled stale. Kyle took the same locker as last year; I picked one on the opposite wall, beside Solomon. The room was noisy, with metal

doors opening and closing, and plastic cleats c
the cement floor.

Solomon glanced over at Kyle and muttered
under his breath, "Another season for Team Saint-\

I was sure he wasn't the only guy who felt that

The season schedule was taped to the chalkboard
opened with Livingston and faced Oradell at midsea
in addition to playing home and away games against ea
of the other seven Suburban Conference schools: Dayto
West Orange, Verona, New Providence, and, our three
main rivals, Caldwell, Madison, and Summit. The season
finished with the Essex County tournament on the last
weekend of October, and the Group III state tournament
the weekend after.

But the specifics of the schedule were irrelevant—
Millburn was simply not allowed to lose. Modestly successful in the decade before, Coach George Alban eventually
built the town's soccer program into a state powerhouse.
In the last season before he retired, Millburn compiled a
22–1 record and a number three final ranking, the only
loss coming in double-overtime of the state championship
game. A banner honoring that team was suspended above
the locker room doorway, reminding every player who
followed that the Millburn program was expected to remain on par with Wall, Kearny, St. Benedict's, and Delran
as the finest in New Jersey.

After putting in my cup and taping my shin guards, I

followed Kyle out of the locker room. On the field, guys were warming up, some passing or dribbling, others stretching. Pennyweather, in his blue shorts and short-sleeved white shirt with MILLBURN SOCCER embroidered on both, walked among the players. Though I saw Pennyweather almost every day of the school year, today he looked uneasy and a bit older than the ten months that had passed since the last time he was on a soccer field—standing dejectedly at the end of last season.

A perfect conference record did nothing to lessen the sting of a 1–0 loss to Columbia High in last year's county title game. That was followed, a week later, by a crushing overtime defeat by Rahway in the Group III state finals, a game that Millburn should've won. Kyle's header off a free kick late in the second half, that would've sealed the game, was disallowed by an awful (and incorrect) offside call. Four minutes later, Rahway tied the score, then eventually won on penalty kicks.

But even before that loss, there had been rumors that the Millburn soccer powers-that-be were not pleased. Maybe it was time for a change. They had had Pennyweather hired; they could have him fired. Often during pep talks, Pennyweather would remind the team that there was a target on its back, making it sound like a badge of honor. What I thought he really meant was that the target was on *his* back.

This season, it'd be worse. Newspaper articles. Cable

TV coverage. College admissions. Scholarships. Parents' egos. Players' egos. It would all come colliding together in the next two and a half months.

"Hustle up, fellas!" Pennyweather shouted.

"Yeah, hustle up, homo," Maako said, running up behind me. He knocked me with his shoulder.

"Gain some weight over the summer, Maako?" I sneered.

"Good one, faggy Fehey," he said, his words punctuated with mock laughter. "Ready for another season watching me from the bench?"

Maako sprinted to the sideline, hollering, "Let's go, Millburn! Time for practice!" He started dribbling a ball around the field, making a big show of himself. I watched each step he took, each touch on the ball.

I wanted to put my cleat up his ass.

COME ON, TONY!" PENNYWEATHER SHOUTED. "Push your-self!"

A week into the season, Pennyweather was trying to break us down. After two hours of exercises and drills, he had the team running the "snake," single file down the sideline, across the end line, up the opposite sideline, then along the far end line. Over and over.

I focused on the back of Kyle's jersey. I didn't let my mind stray. I couldn't afford to. One step after the other, constant and continuous. One breath after the other, constant and continuous. Gallo came up hard, sprinting to the outside of the snake. I could hear the ragged breaths of our striker, Pete Beuhler, behind me and our collective steps pounding the ground.

"That's it," Pennyweather shouted. "Keep going!"

As we rounded the corner, Gallo settled into the front position and Pennyweather called for the next man. Richie Luongo, our right winger, took off from the end, passing Pete, then me, then Kyle, then goalkeeper Stuart Masterson, as he charged up the sideline. My turn was coming. I had to bust it. Here was a chance to show Pennyweather that, late in practice, with puke at the back of my throat, I wouldn't let the snake beat me.

Richie soon settled into the front position.

"Nice job!" Pennyweather said. "Glad to see some of you worked hard this summer! Pete, go!"

Pete, who had been struggling to keep pace, shot past me, then Kyle. I was now last in line. My heart couldn't possibly beat any harder, waiting for Pennyweather to call my name. I had to sprint to the lead position as fast as possible. The more time it took, the longer I had to run and the more grueling my turn was for the team.

Pete was quickly fading. Pennyweather was yelling. Guys in line were groaning.

Pete slowed.

Then stopped.

And booted his guts.

"Awww, that's what I'm talking about," Pennyweather

said. "We might as well toss that preseason ranking in the crapper. Only nine teams better than us in the state? I'll bet there are ninety teams better than us. Fehey!"

I looked up.

"Waiting for a goddamn invitation?" Pennyweather snapped.

My cleats dug into the grass as I overtook Kyle, then Stuart. I felt my body fighting me. My rib cage tightened and my calves stiffened. My mind was dizzy, but I had to keep it together. I ran by a few more guys. Richie, at the front of the snake setting the pace, still seemed a mile away. Falling to the side would've been bliss. I wouldn't have been the first. Shawn had done it early on; Pete just a few moments ago.

That's exactly what Pennyweather was expecting. I passed Maako. My legs kept churning, though my ankles and feet were going numb. I gritted my teeth, my breaths sounding like angry hisses. I moved up the snake.

Closer . . .

And closer . . .

Richie was right there . . .

And then he was behind me, and I was at the lead. I wanted to drop, but I wouldn't let that happen. It was an impressive display, Pennyweather had to agree. I'd made a statement. Mark it down, Pennyweather! Mark it on that damn clipboard of yours! I'm not riding the bench all season. I'm gonna play. I'm gonna score goals. I'm gonna taste the glory that Kyle thinks he has a divine right to. I raised my eyes to the center of the field. *Look at me, Pennyweather, look at me!*

"Okay, Kyle, show 'em how it's done," Pennyweather said.

Within a short time, Kyle was in front of me. We continued around the field, lap after lap, hearing Pennyweather bark out commands, but not really listening. Just waiting for another preseason practice to come to an end.

THE GARAGE LIGHTS BEHIND ME stretched a long shadow down our driveway. I had a garbage can in each hand, my mind lost in thoughts about soccer and senior year and a million other things, when something in the dark caught my attention. I looked up. Kyle was crossing his front lawn. I was sure he saw me, but he didn't say a word. I didn't say anything, either. I set the garbage cans at the edge of the street, and our game of charades continued.

After practice, I'd overheard guys talking about a party at the circle. Gallo asked Kyle if he'd be there. And Solomon. Pete and Dennis, too. No one asked me if I'd be there. Not that I expected anyone to. It was such a fucked-up contradiction. I wasn't exactly banned from these parties. I mean, there wouldn't be a posted sign, saying, YOU HAVE TO BE *THIS* HIGH ON THE LADDER TO ENTER. But I wouldn't be invited, either. It was all unspoken, yet made so perfectly clear. We could share the same soccer field and locker room, and we could share the same school and classrooms, but we weren't equals.

I looked down Lake Road, but Kyle's silhouette had disappeared. "Thanks." I felt like saying it loud enough for him to hear. "Thanks a helluva lot."

Inside the house, I climbed the stairs to my bedroom. I closed the door and turned the lock. On my dresser sat a half-dozen college applications. My life was neatly summed up: seventeen years old, varsity soccer team member, ninety-second percentile on the SAT, three AP classes, essay questions, and a photograph. Admissions people would pat themselves on the back for assessing whether I'd "enrich" their campus. It was all such a joke. They couldn't possibly know me from essays or grades or test scores. They couldn't get inside me. They saw only what they wanted to see. Experience one day *as* Jonathan Fehey. Then maybe they'd understand a tiny bit.

I took off my jeans and shirt. In my closet, I swept aside a dozen hangers of shirts and pants, and stepped through. I bent down to move away a wooden chest. My fingers reached along the wall for a seam, then followed that seam to a latch. I unhooked the latch and pushed open a small door. I then closed it behind me.

Inside the attic, I stood up. Heat and humidity, trapped under the roof all day, swallowed me. The space was pitch-black and insulated, and the pungent smell of mothballs and bare floorboards filled my head. I took in a deep breath, filling my lungs with the sweltering, musty air. Prickly sensations raced up and down my body.

Soon, sweat started to rise on my forehead.

And my arms.

Across my back.

And along my stomach.

This was my place to be alone. To let my thoughts run wild. To feel whatever I wanted to feel. In solitude. But more than just solitude. In a kind of cocoon, closed off from the world outside.

▫▫▫▫

In the attic, I liked to remember her.

Ruby Luvelle.

I met Ruby last summer on a teen tour through Cleveland, Chicago, and Sioux City, eventually stopping in Vail at a ski resort turned quiet for the summer. She wore her frizzy brown hair pulled back in a ponytail, listened to the Divinyls all the time, and had a half-dozen piercings on her ears.

"Where're you from?" I asked.

"Nowhere," she said with a shrug. "And everywhere."

Ruby actually came from a town near Worcester, Massachusetts, and was a thousand times better looking than I deserved. But she chose me when she could've picked any of the other guys on the tour. With Ruby I had a clean slate. No ladder. No circle. No crowd. No one pulling her aside to ask what she was doing with faggy Fehey.

We spent days sitting next to each other on the bus and hanging out on our own at tour stops. I told her how I was the star of my high school soccer team, planning on going to UVA on a full athletic scholarship. About pinpoint passes that I never made, shots I never took, spectacular goals I never scored. Ruby never questioned anything I said. She'd look at me with her marble brown eyes and whisper, as if inside my head, "Jonathan, it'd be wicked cool to watch you play."

On our last night, while everyone else went to the movies, Ruby and I snuck into another hotel and made our way to the rooftop pool. We sat alone in the Jacuzzi, chlorine foam bubbling on the water's surface, our hands exploring below. We talked about silly stuff, but everything that mattered. Ruby wanted me to visit her before soccer season started. She said we shared something. Simpatico, she called it.

Later, we buried ourselves under a pile of towels on a chaise longue, staring up at a black sky dusted with a zillion stars, sharing a bottle of cheap wine. Ruby told me about the summer house that her family had on Lake

Winnipesaukee in New Hampshire and how, two years ago, her friend drowned one night swimming alone. "He was wicked drunk," she said. "He just got tired." That's why she didn't swim in lakes or ponds or oceans anymore. She didn't like going near any of them, either.

I was going to tell her about my favorite place—the edge of the dock on South Pond with the afternoon sun beating down, dragonflies buzzing, the water's surface glimmering—but I didn't think I should. Sometimes you can't be honest with someone even when you want to be dead-on honest. But I did tell Ruby, when she asked, that remembering things about my dad was like "trying to catch a leaf in a wind storm." The words just sort of came to me. She thought I was lyrical.

"What about your mom?" she asked.

"She's pretty cool," I said. "It's only me and her, though. It's been that way a long time."

"So what happened to your dad?" she asked. But before I could say anything, she said, "No, you don't have to tell me. That's just me being super nosy. Know where my mom is? In Houston, on business. Dad's in San Fran. I'll see them both on Friday in Taos. It'll be the first time in, like, months." She rolled her eyes. "They wanna fly home as a *family*."

I didn't have to say a word; Ruby just kept talking. She was good at that. "That's why I'm on this damn trip. They send me every summer to some place or another." She reached her hand out to me. "Oh, I didn't mean it that way. This trip's been wicked great. Really, I swear. I just don't know why they bother playing games. They hate each other—I mean hate, with a capital H. I know it. Our family knows it. Their friends know it. Even *my* friends know it. Supposedly they named me after that Stones song when they were young and blissfully in love. Now? They make such a big deal of trying to put up a good front. Guess I shouldn't let it bother me, but they're either up my ass trying to know everything about my life, or they don't give a damn because they're all caught up in their own shit. I can't deal with it sometimes, know what I mean?"

Ruby stopped, as if she was done spilling her frustration. Then she said something that blew me away. "Jonathan, let's do it."

"Do what?" I said.

"Knock boots, mess around—whatever you wanna call it." She grinned. "Come on, I wanna *be* with you."

I stared at her. Blankly, I'm sure. I wondered if this was a genuine moment of outrageous fortune, or had my ears deceived me in a colossally cruel way.

"Okay, how about this?" she said. "I request the opportunity to make love to the hot soccer stud, Jonathan Fehey. That sound better?"

I looked around. But before I could answer, Ruby's legs were straddling me. She touched her forehead to mine and let her hair cascade down around us, blocking out the little bit of light there was on the rooftop. It felt like our minds were in a warm, tight space. My body tingled from the heat of her skin. I breathed in her scent deeply so that I'd never forget it.

"Relax, Jonathan," she said, her fingernails slow dancing down my chest . . . Then my stomach. "You're gonna have a wicked good time."

Something inside me was certain—absolutely certain—that it wasn't luck, but my destiny to be with Ruby, alone, poolside, on top of this hotel, feeling her body on top of my chest, then melting over me. Her mouth found mine and we didn't stop kissing until later, though I couldn't remember the time, or how much of it had passed, or anything else in the world.

▫ ▫ ▫ ▫

I was sweating, really sweating, perspiration not even beading on my skin but simply rising from the pores and spreading. Down my forehead. My back. Down my stomach. And my thighs. I lowered my arms, and the tracks of sweat went *drip, drip, drip* on the stained attic floorboards beneath me.

▫ ▫ ▫ ▫

Ruby and I hid in a storage closet in the basement of the hotel. We figured no one would find us behind the metal shelves of tools, old signs, discarded linens, pairs of work boots, and maintenance jump suits with the hotel logo on the back. We placed two chairs facing each other and sat with our legs intertwined. Ruby talked and talked; then we'd lean forward to kiss, and sit back and smile. She told me about her brother, Eugene, a sophomore majoring in geology at the University of Minnesota. They spoke on the phone once a week. She said she thought about applying to Carleton College to be in the same state with him, but the school didn't really fit her.

"I wanna go to Wellesley," Ruby said. "I'll live in a residence hall for my first couple of years, then get a place in Cambridge. I take the T to Back Bay almost every weekend during school anyway. There's so much I can show you. And my friends, Marcie and Donna, are the best. You'll like them. They'll think you're adorable, like I do."

It was late and I was tired. But it was a soft tired, a comforting tired—nothing like being tired from running the snake or listening to Pennyweather or fighting Kyle for a loose ball. It was the kind of tired the luckiest guy in the world would enjoy. I slept well that night, long and heavy.

From the moment I woke up the next morning, all I could think about was Ruby and what we had done. It wasn't that it was wrong—far from it—it just seemed that I had crossed a kind of threshold. Something was different. Like I was suddenly grown up, but at the same time kind of embarrassed, too. Yet whatever uncertainty spun in my head, it all disappeared the moment Ruby climbed the stairs of the tour bus.

"What's up, Jonathan?" she said before kissing me on the lips.

I remember wishing that we had been in the middle of the high school cafeteria at noon, when people from every grade were there eating. On the tour bus, I heard the surprised whispers and felt the envious stares, but Ruby was so sure of herself. She touched her hand to mine. She told me how wicked cool last night was, and while a part of me wasn't sure whether to believe her totally, the rest of me was ready to combust.

"You'll write?" Ruby asked, as the bus headed to Denver. "Because I really like to write letters. Long letters. Long letters that go on and on and on telling you what I'm thinking and doing and wondering." She tilted her head and said, "I like to get them, too, Jonathan."

I told her I liked to write letters, even though I didn't really. (Again, you can't always be honest.) We exchanged addresses. Ruby encircled hers in a heart. She made me promise to write every week. Then she looked at my address and her expression turned curious.

"You're from Short Hills?" she said. "In Jersey?"

I nodded.

"No way," she said. "My cousin lives there. On my mom's side. You might know her. Sloan Ruehl."

My heart sank. As a freshman and sophomore—even before the creation of the ladder—Sloan Ruehl had been firmly entrenched in the hierarchy of our grade. She enjoyed making life miserable for anyone she thought wasn't in her realm of greatness. I told Ruby about her cousin and all the people at school she left in her wake. It didn't surprise Ruby.

"Sloan always was kind of bitchy," she said. "I love her, though. Know what? I'm gonna call her and say you and I did it, like, ten times. That'll give you a good rep."

"But we didn't," I said.

Ruby smiled. "Then we'll have to when you visit. Or," she said, "when I visit Sloan for fall break."

Was Ruby going to lift me from obscurity at Millburn and make me someone no one thought I was? Was she going to confer on me a kind of seal of approval by telling Sloan and, in effect, the entire school, that we had *been* together? Was my existence at Millburn going to suddenly change, so that I was on par with the very crowd I envied so much?

I wanted to be popular—who didn't? But I wasn't a star athlete. I was smart, but just one in a class of smart people. My mom wasn't rich. My dad wasn't around. Whatever my looks were, it didn't matter. The ladder had ensured that the prospects for my junior and senior year would be dim. Was I suddenly going to grow taller? Doubtful. Or become a soccer stud? Unlikely. Junior and senior years lay ahead of me—two long years of frustration. Maybe I could convince my mom to move. She had been thinking about it. Maybe to Mendham or Mountain Lakes or Flemington. That was my best chance for escape.

Until Ruby.

She was going to change my life—after she had *already* changed my life—so that I could walk the school hallway, looking at those less worthy as those in the crowd had looked at me.

It made for an impossibly long flight home from Denver. In the margins of a magazine I made a list of how things would be different, what parties would be like at the circle. A new life opened up. A magnificent one, one made up of dreams busting from my mind. Nothing was going to stop me from claiming my rightful place at Millburn.

And it all came back to Ruby, the girl from Worcester who was all I wished to be. I knew we were together only a week or so and that we shared each other just one night, but did you need more than that to fall in love? Did you need a certain amount of time to know that person is someone you envied, but wished to be like even more? I didn't think so. Ruby was that opportunity that comes only when God is shining down on you, a rare occurrence that had to be taken for all it was worth.

Thirty thousand feet above Michigan . . . Lake Erie . . . Pennsylvania . . . and eventually northern Jersey, I dreamed of my upcoming junior year. I figured the letters from Ruby might come early and often. Then slow. Then eventually stop. But she would have done all that was needed. I'd have status, I'd *be* someone. I don't remember my mom picking me up from Newark Airport or the ride home, but I remember being so sure about how things were going to change.

But Ruby never made it to Taos.

Thirty miles into New Mexico, on Route 285 South, the bus driver momentarily lost control on the rain-slick highway, and the Greyhound skidded sideways before righting itself and slamming into the back of an eighteen-wheeler. Seven of the forty-two passengers had injuries that put them in the hospital. One didn't make it.

It was a quirky thing. One in a million. The impact came as Ruby was reaching for her backpack above her seat, sending her into the aisle backwards. She hit the base of the dashboard. Fatal head and neck trauma.

And that was that.

I was told about the accident a few days later when I called Ruby's home number. Through tears, her mother explained what had happened. "I'm sorry," I said. It was all I could manage. Her mother thanked me, and we hung up.

At school, I wanted to say something to Sloan. One afternoon, early last fall, she and I were in algebra class alone, both of us finding ways to occupy time before the others arrived instead of having to acknowledge each other's presence. It was the kind of moment that, in years past, Sloan wouldn't have let go by without saying whatever nasty thing came into her mind. But not that day. She checked her notebook once.

Twice.

Three times.

Glanced at the clock.

Then out the classroom window.

I wanted to tell Sloan that I knew her cousin and that she was the most incredible girl I had ever met, that I would ever meet. I wanted to tell her that her cousin really liked me. I wanted to tell her that I had been inside her cousin one night, but she would be inside me forever. I wanted to say that she should bring me into the crowd, because her cousin Ruby would've said so.

I wanted to say a lot of things, but I didn't.

◻◻◻◻

I felt lightheaded, and spat into the dark of the attic. What was the point of remembering? When I remembered

Ruby, it tore me up inside, knowing I'd never be able to relive that week with her again. And as the memories ran through my mind, they only reinforced that the past was over. Gone. I was left feeling hollow, wondering if that week had even been worth living in the first place.

I didn't want to face this. I just wanted to come down slowly; I didn't want to crash. But things couldn't be that simple. I felt trapped in the attic, just as I felt trapped at Millburn High. Both were oppressive. But I could leave the attic. I could step in and out when I wanted. It didn't have a hold on me, other than the one I allowed. And so, it was a way for me to escape my reality and be who I wanted, and go where I wanted, and do all I could imagine. The ladder, on the other hand, was the ball and chain that kept me in my place with the people at school. It was out of my control. I never asked to be on the rung I was. But I was hung there nonetheless.

I crawled back through the attic door. The air in my bedroom felt cool on my sweaty skin. I grabbed a towel, dried off, then sat at the end of my bed. I looked toward the window, wondering what Kyle was doing, what girls he was hanging with. I thought I heard voices, laughing and joking. But my mind was teasing me. The circle was certainly too far away. Much too far.

Pᴇɴɴʏᴡᴇᴀᴛʜᴇʀ sᴛᴏᴏᴅ ᴀᴛ ᴛʜᴇ ᴄᴇɴᴛᴇʀ ᴄɪʀᴄʟᴇ, jotting down notes on a clipboard, a duffel bag at his feet. The JVs were sitting in the stands. I looked around the field. New lime had been laid down on the sidelines and end lines, and flags marked each of the four corners. Something was definitely up.

"Bring it in, fellas," Pennyweather said.

The varsity team gathered around him. On Pennyweather's cue, the scoreboard lit up.

ʜᴏᴍᴇ 0 ᴀᴡᴀʏ 0 15:00.

"This is the roster we're going to war with," he said, his eyes sweeping over each player. "From this moment until mid-November, Millburn Soccer is your life. You go to sleep with Millburn Soccer on your mind. You have dreams about Millburn Soccer. You wake up hungry for Millburn Soccer. Everyone expects you to go undefeated. Newspapers do. Opponents do. The town does. That doesn't leave any margin for error. So I'm not gonna waste any time waiting for you guys to get in game shape. We're going all-out today."

A man wearing black shorts and a black and white striped shirt jogged in from the parking lot. "You remember Mr. Scolari," Pennyweather said, gesturing to our old junior high gym teacher. "He'll be refereeing today."

Pennyweather grabbed an armful of jerseys from the duffel bag. "We're scrimmaging. White versus blue. White'll be the home team." He tossed a white game jersey to each player as he called out their names. "Stuart in goal. Maako, sweeper. Jones and Solomon, fullbacks. Maynard, stopper. Midfielders, Brad, Kyle, and Dennis. Wingers, Gallo, and Richie. Pete, striker."

I waited among the others, stretching my legs to ease my nerves. It was starters versus backups. Them against us. Bright scoreboard lights. New lime. A uniformed referee. JVs watching from the stands. This was serious. I glanced at Kyle. He had his game face on.

"The blue team . . ." Pennyweather named the goalie, defenders, midfielders, and wingers. Each guy grabbed a blue jersey and slipped it on. Finally, Pennyweather said, "Fehey, striker."

I took my jersey and sprinted into position. The few guys left took seats on the varsity bench.

"Let's make one thing clear, fellas," Pennyweather said. "No one's spot in the starting lineup is set in stone."

But we all knew better. There was no way the blue team was going to win—we were going up against Kyle, Maako, and Brad, for God's sake. And if the blue team did win, so what? Pennyweather wasn't going to dump the entire starting team for backups.

Still, every practice, every drill, every lap was a chance to let Pennyweather know that my skills had improved since last season, and that I was sure as hell ready to contribute more than just giving a first-stringer a breather a couple times a game.

"Who's gonna show me something today?" Pennyweather said. He turned and walked off the field. "Get yourselves organized. Mr. Scolari will blow the whistle."

◻◻◻◻

"Fehey." Maako laughed. "Have ya even *touched* the ball yet?"

A striker's job was to score goals; a sweeper's job was to stop that from happening. Maako was doing his job infinitely better than I was doing mine. Halfway through the third quarter, the white team led 2–0 on a goal by Pete off a scramble in the penalty area and another on a direct kick from Kyle. Most of the play had been inside the blue defensive zone, where our back line struggled against Kyle and his midfield control. The few times the ball did come my way, Maako was there to shut down the threat. On both sides of the field, our blue team looked every bit like a bunch of second-stringers—unorganized and overmatched.

"Didja hear me, Fehey?" Maako taunted.

"I'll get my chances."

"Gee, ya think?" Maako said. "Before the game ends?"

"Drop dead, Maako."

"Good comeback. Think of that all by yourself, or did ya have to get permission from Kyle?"

The ball came up the sideline.

"Don't bother," Maako said, shadowing me. He was fast, insanely strong, and had an overwhelming arrogance that made it clear that if you and he were in a battle to get a loose ball, he expected to win every time.

But I saw an opening. "Through, through!" I called out to a blue teammate.

I heard Maako's footsteps behind me as we chased the pass into the corner. With my back against him, I gained control, pushing the ball forward and backwards, waiting for my wingers to move into our offensive zone. But while I was looking and thinking, Maako knocked me off balance with his elbow, then cut in front to steal possession.

With a few quick strides, he opened up space between us. I tried to catch him, but he passed the ball to Solomon, who one-timed it to Kyle at the center circle. And just like that, the white team was on the attack again.

As I jogged by, Maako said, "Fehey, just take a seat on the bench. The two of you are such close friends."

◻◻◻◻

The scoreboard clock showed 00:00. Mr. Scolari blew his whistle to end the game. Final score, 5–0.

I ripped off my jersey and tossed it at the duffel bag. It had been a long, lousy sixty minutes of Maako making me look like a goddamn JV. I wanted to get out of there, but Pennyweather started with another of his inane pep talks, reminding the team that no one was guaranteed a spot in the starting lineup when we had all just experienced why the eleven players on the white team were pegged for first string, while the rest of us remained scrubs.

When Pennyweather was done, I said to Kyle, "I'll be at your car," and I started toward the school parking lot.

◻◻◻◻

I slammed the garage door shut, put on the stereo, and cranked the volume. I dropped a soccer ball to the cement floor, nudged it forward with my sneaker, then let loose a shot. The ball banged against the inside of the wood garage door, careening back to me.

Again, I reached my right foot back and drilled another shot. One after the other. Right foot. Left foot. Each time the ball smacked the door, shaking the metal runners that ran along the ceiling. Each time I imagined Maako's face taking the full impact of the ball.

Five blistering shots.

Then ten.

Then twenty.

The music was thundering and the garage door was shaking and the runners were clanking, and all I wished for was one of my shots to bring down the whole damn garage. When I looked up, my mom was standing in the doorway. I turned off the stereo.

"Who're you mad at?" she asked.

"Just practicing," I said.

"Didn't you have practice earlier?"

"I need more work," I said. "I need *a lot* more work."

My mom didn't push it. "Well, we really can't afford to have you break the garage door," she said with a muted smile. "Maybe you can get 'more work' another way."

"Sure, Ma," I said.

▢▢▢▢

I threw on my sneakers. My body was tired, but my mind was wired. I started down Lake Road, still pissed off about Maako. How was he able to dog me so badly in the scrimmage? I had to remember his strength. His speed. His quickness. I had to remember that obnoxiously smug look on his face. I wanted it to be branded in my brain so that Maako—or anyone else—would never beat me like that again.

My sneakers pounded against the pavement as I passed between North and South ponds. Up ahead, Lake Road arced to the right and crossed over Redemption Bridge. I thought I could see a girl with willowy, light brown hair on the other side. My feet suddenly didn't feel quite as heavy.

As I got closer, I could see she had a delicate face, soft eyes, and an odd habit of walking with her forearm across her waist. I slowed down. The girl glanced at me. There was something familiar about her. Our eyes locked. I realized then she was the girl who had been sitting with Trinity and Stephanie underneath the bridge a few weeks earlier.

With a flick of her hand, she waved. *"Ciao."*

Chow? What was that supposed to mean?

I nodded to the girl—like I would to a teammate. A moment after I did, I knew how stupid that must've looked. And a moment after that, I was past her.

My stomach fluttered and my thoughts were going a

mile a minute. Should I turn around? What would I say? Would she stop? She probably didn't know who I was. Or worse, knowing my luck, Trinity and Stephanie had already told her everything about me—at least, everything they thought they knew. I looked over my shoulder, almost tripping over my feet, but the girl had already crossed Redemption Bridge and was continuing up Lake Road.

My run slowed to a halfhearted jog. I tried to reignite the anger I had for Maako, but my mind was distracted. Forget about the scrimmage. Forget about Maako. Forget about getting my ass whipped. There'd be other practices to obsess over. I stopped and sat on the curb. All I could think about was this pretty girl walking farther and farther away.

I WAS GLAD TO BE done lifting weights. Benches, curls, deadlifts—that was my Saturday night. There was a party going on in town, but I didn't know where. Not that it mattered. That was for Kyle and other people.

Between sets, I thought about the girl on Lake Road. Maybe she was sleeping over at Stephanie's tonight. I tried to come up with an excuse to knock on the Saint-Claires' door, but it was much too late. Maybe tomorrow I'd see her leaving the house from my bedroom window. Maybe then I'd run outside and say hello.

I closed the basement door, turned off the kitchen lights, and climbed the stairs to the second floor. The television was on in my mom's bedroom.

"Jonny, could you come here a second?" she called.

I stood at the doorway. My mom was sitting upright on the bed, with a checkbook and bills spread out in front of her. She took off her glasses and placed them on the nightstand. "Did you lock up?"

"Yeah."

"And the lights?"

"All off."

"I bought the notebooks and pens you need for school," she said. "They're on the kitchen table."

"Thanks," I said.

"I'm going to need your help around the house on Saturday," she said. I guess I didn't look particularly thrilled, because my mom shrugged and gave me a sympathetic look. "There's no one else but us, Jonny."

I understood. I turned to leave but stopped. "Uh, Ma, do you know what the word 'chow' means? I'm not sure how to spell it."

"*Ciao,*" she said. "It's Italian."

"Italian?"

"It means hello, or goodbye."

"Oh," I said. "How do you know which one?"

"Depends on the situation," she said. "You have to figure out what the person meant. Why?"

"No reason," I said. "I heard it somewhere. On a TV show, I think. I was wondering, that's all. I'm gonna go to sleep. Good night."

"*Ciao,* Jonny," she said with a curious smile.

I SLAPPED THE ALARM CLOCK off. Morning sunlight angled through my bedroom-window curtains.

"Damn . . ." I muttered.

My hope for an instantaneous skip in time to graduation day had been an exercise in futility. As had my more modest wish for a freakish thunderstorm to tear down trees and power lines and flood the high school grounds.

I sat up, feeling a twinge in my lower back and stiffness in my knees. It was soccer season—I couldn't have expected to feel any better. A short-sleeved shirt and tan pants were folded on my desk chair; shoes were lined up below. I peed, took a shower, and, a short time later, sat at the kitchen table eating a bagel with cream cheese.

And so began the countdown of days, weeks, and months until I'd escape Millburn High for a college somewhere far away.

Outside, Kyle beeped his car horn.

"Gotta go, Ma," I said, putting the dish in the sink. "See ya later." My mind was already out the door.

"Wait a second," she called out. "Wait just one second."

My mom and I didn't have to make this some grand bon voyage. Later tonight there'd be time to answer questions about classes and teachers. Besides, there'd be plenty of other school mornings. One hundred and seventy-nine to be exact.

My mom rushed down the stairs, buttoning her blouse and straightening her skirt as she entered the kitchen. "You look very nice," she said.

"Thanks for putting my clothes out," I said. "How 'bout we go back to me doing it myself, okay?"

She smiled and nodded. "First day of senior year. How do you feel?"

"Like crap."

"Language, young man." She wrapped her arms around me. "Nervous?"

"Ma, please." I started to pull away, but she held tight.

"I wake up one morning," she said wistfully, "and I've gone from being a teenager dreaming of making the Weequahic High cheerleading squad, to a wife and mother. I wake up another morning and my son—that little boy with the runny nose I always had to wipe—is all grown up."

"Kyle's waiting," I said.

"He'll wait a little longer," she said. "You think your mom's a little crazy, don't you? You'll understand when you have a son."

"Tomorrow will be like today," I said, opening the front door, then adding, "Thursday will be like tomorrow," as it closed behind me.

I could see Kyle tapping his fingers on the steering wheel. I jumped down the front portico steps, jogged across our lawn, and opened the passenger door. Stephanie, sitting in the back seat, greeted me with a disinterested pout. She was wearing thick makeup, painted-on black jeans that hung well below her belly button, and a black tube top across her chest. Trinity's influence was unmistakable. I climbed in.

"Ready?" Kyle said.

"As I'll ever be."

Kyle cranked the stereo and gunned the engine. The BMW spun out until the tires caught hold of the pavement. He went from first to fourth gear in the blink of an eye, his arm jerking backwards, then forward, then back again.

The car rumbled over Redemption Bridge, then down Highland Avenue, taking the curve around the Racquets Club like a Matchbox car on a grooved plastic track. Twice over the summer, Kyle had been pulled over by Millburn police for speeding; twice he got off with just a warning after they recognized him. People at school thought it was only a matter of time before he got into an accident, but I never worried, confident God would never take away one of his best.

I heard Stephanie snapping her gum. "Must be feeling lucky today," I said.

"Lucky?" she said. "For what?"

"Your first day of high school and you get a ride with two seniors."

"Yeah, sure," Stephanie said. "I'll be the envy of all the sophomore girls. They'll say, 'Ohmygod, ohmygod, you rode to school with Jonny Fehey. Tell us, please please please, what's he like?'"

I looked over my shoulder.

Stephanie smirked, pulling down the top of her jeans with a long black fingernail. "Snap a pic, Jonny; it'll last longer."

Stephanie was going to fit in perfectly at Millburn High. That was a shame. She used to be a sweet girl living at the edge of her brother's world, as happy stomping in puddles after a summer downpour as she was prancing through leaf piles on fall afternoons. But by junior high, Stephanie had become a frequent visitor to detention hall. Now it was clear she wanted to step out from Kyle's shadow—at least as much as a sophomore girl could when her big brother was the school's star athlete—while Trinity would be right in front of her to lead the way.

Kyle turned into the school driveway, banking left in front of the main entrance, past the gymnasium. He lowered the stereo, and his fingers stopped tapping. I think he noticed Maako walk by; I certainly did. Kyle followed the line of cars into the parking lot, taking the best of the prime spaces set aside for seniors.

Stephanie reached her hand out. "I need money," she said. "For lunch."

"Mom didn't give you any?" Kyle said.

"Just give me some. You don't want me anorexic, do ya?"

Someone knocked on the trunk. Trinity and the girl from Redemption Bridge walked by. My stomach swirled.

"Who's that?" I said to Stephanie.

She shook her head, dismissively. "The sweet aroma of sophomore girls arousing the carnivores. Pathetic, just pathetic."

Kyle slapped a ten-dollar bill in her hand. "You owe me."

"As the younger sibling of the famous Kyle Saint-Claire, I owe you for every day of my life," Stephanie said. "I just thank God for being part of your gene pool."

"It's your first day," Kyle said. "Try not to get in

trouble—Mom and Dad don't need the hassle. Most important—and get this through your thick skull—don't embarrass me. Now leave, wiseass."

"Stephanie, who's that?" I said again.

She squeezed out from behind my seat, giving me another why-are-you-talking-to-me look. "The new girl."

"What's her name?"

"The. New. Girl. No need for you to know anything else, Jonny-boy," Stephanie said. She called out to Trinity, who offered a quick wave but never broke stride.

□□□□

The school was loud and frenzied, churning with juniors and seniors seeing friends for the first time since last June, and sophomores, with their deer-in-the-headlights looks, searching for homerooms. Kyle and I moved along with the flow of traffic, then parted ways. He went down one hallway, high-fiving and slapping hands with guys on the team, while I went down another.

The fresh faces. The excitement. For a second, I thought something *did* feel different, like I was somehow taller, or more mature. Maybe my mom was right. I was a *senior.* Maybe that had more status than I realized. I'd play in most of our games and, hopefully, chalk up a few goals and assists. Some decent college would accept me.

Fall and winter would pass, then spring, and before I knew it, my time at Millburn High would come to a quiet, if not pleasant, end.

Piece of cake.

But seeing Sloan Ruehl smacked me back to reality. She stood by an open locker, surrounded by the group of girls people at school called her "band of bitches." One of them would say something, then wait for Sloan to smile or frown, laugh or shake her head, smirk or roll her eyes. Then they'd all do the same.

Sloan was at the top of our class and the top of the ladder. She was pretty, privileged, and had a reputation for drinking like a fish. It was well known that she started last year's ritual of Friday liquid lunches—a can of Diet Coke spiked with Bacardi—that ended abruptly when one of her bitches passed out in chemistry class.

At the other end of the hallway, I noticed Abigail Blonski walking our way. People thought Abigail was fat. Most called her a dog. Last year, she and I were assigned an AP bio class project together. I thought she was quirky (in a good way) and kind of funny. She planned on going to FIT for fashion merchandising. But none of that mattered. Abigail surely hung from one of the lowest rungs.

Abigail must've seen Sloan, because she immediately moved to the opposite side of the hallway, trying to be as inconspicuous as possible, eyes down. Yet when she got close, Sloan's bitches turned in her direction.

"Fatty," one of them sneered. Another hissed something about her clothes, or her acne, or whatever deficiency du jour they wanted to mock. Then they all burst out laughing. People stopped and stared.

Abigail hurried down the hallway past me.

"Are you all right?" I said to her, but she didn't look my way. I wanted to say something more, but she had already disappeared into the stairwell.

It was my turn to pass through the gauntlet.

I stared at Sloan, expecting a look of disgust to spread across her face as a very real indication that I had deluded myself into thinking this year would be any different from last year. Sloan looked at me, too. But, strangely, there wasn't contempt or nastiness on her face. Even her bitches seemed to quiet. As I walked by, Sloan's lips parted like she was going to say something—or maybe I just imagined it.

"I miss Ruby," I wanted to tell her.

But my mouth didn't move.

I don't know why.

I thought a lot about Ruby. All the time. I had just two photographs in my bedroom. One of my mom and me at Great Adventure on my twelfth birthday; the other, a Polaroid of Ruby the day I left for Denver's airport. I remembered everything about her—her voice, her laugh, her whisper, her scent. They would always be with me.

I wondered whether I really wanted to let Sloan know how much I missed her cousin, or if it was just something

that needed to come from my mouth and be heard by
the only person at Millburn who might understand what
it meant.

I looked over my shoulder; she glanced over hers.

The distance between us increased.

From an arm's length, to a few yards.

To the length of the hallway.

A SMALL SCRATCH IN the metal shelf marked where I had started.

I had thumbed through hundreds of books. Thick ones. Thin ones. Tall ones. Short ones. Sometimes I'd turn the pages slowly to make certain. Other times I'd fan the pages quickly because I just didn't care anymore (even though I really did). The rumor was the ladder had been drawn on a sheet of graph paper, then slipped inside a book's front cover. Or tucked inside a back cover. Or hidden somewhere in between.

One Sunday every month or so, I borrowed my mom's car to drive to the Millburn library. All the librarians knew me. I think they thought I was one of those responsible students, spending his time finishing homework for the upcoming week, or diligently researching a term paper. They'd smile when I walked in. I'd say hello, then climb the spiral staircase to the stacks on the second floor.

I returned another handful of books to the shelf, then sat back. I heard the soft murmur of discussions at the reference desk, but otherwise, the library was quiet. I closed my eyes. So many damn books. Row upon row. Shelf upon shelf. Stacks upon stacks. It seemed like it would never end. There were tens of thousands of pages to thumb through, maybe hundreds of thousands. I wondered if this was all just a ridiculous waste of time. Maybe the ladder wasn't hidden here in the first place. Maybe that was the cruel joke—making our class believe the ladder existed when it never really did.

But yet, what if it did exist?

And I found it?

Would I throw it away?

That wouldn't fix much; the damage had been done a year and a half earlier. Or maybe it would. Maybe I'd burn the ladder in a ceremonial fire on the high school lawn so that everyone could see. I'd gladly deal with the consequences. Or maybe I'd change the ladder by mixing up the names—putting my own on one of the highest rungs—then make a hundred copies to spread out on the cafeteria tables, tack up in the hallways, and tape to classroom blackboards. I'd bet that would shatter our grade's hierarchy to smithereens.

I pulled more books from the shelf. I opened the first and flipped through the pages.

One, two, three, four, five, six, seven, eight, nine, ten, eleven . . .

And so on . . .

Soon, that book was done and I was on to the next. And the next after that. Until a pile of books sat at my side and a small scratch could be marked farther down the shelf for the next time.

A STEADY DOWNPOUR KEPT the cafeteria crowded. A half-eaten turkey sandwich and a page of quadratic equations sat in front of me. I looked out the window, watching rain spill over the patio's cement tabletops. Our game against New Providence hadn't been called off; the weather was expected to pass. I hated playing on a soaked field. I hated even more watching the game from a wet bench.

A painted banner stretched across the cafeteria entrance. GO MILLERS! STAY UNDEFEATED! The *Millburn Item* was already making comparisons to the school's best-ever team. To open the season, we crushed Livingston, 5–1, and Dayton, 6–0, then turned a two-goal lead in the first half against West Orange into an 8–2 drubbing. After winning our first six games handily, we climbed to eighth in the state rankings. Against Verona last week, Kyle set the Essex County record for most hat tricks in a career. Afterward, Pennyweather awarded him the game ball—just another to put on the Saint-Claires' crowded living room mantel.

But there was still a long way to go. The significant part of the regular season didn't start until the middle of October—that's when we began play against our three rivals. I think the conference schedule-makers did that on purpose, trying to lull us with weaker opponents in the first two-thirds of the season, then leave win-or-die games for the final third. It wasn't a secret that teams in the conference were tired of seeing Millburn at the top of the standings year in and year out.

My focus returned to the math problems, at least momentarily. I vaguely heard talking around me, but not any particular conversation, and I noticed people moving about, but no one in particular. Then, out of the corner of my eye, I saw the new girl, Annalisa Gianni, walk in.

She was still a curiosity in school; almost everybody knew her name. Her family had moved to Short Hills from Italy. The story was that whatever her father did for work was just a cover for ties to the Sicilian mob. I'd see her in the hallways and watch her coming and going at the Saint-

Claires' house. It seemed she'd found her place as Trinity and Stephanie's *protégé*. Unfortunately, they were going to mold her into someone just like them.

Annalisa brushed the hair off her face and searched for a place to sit. When space opened up at one of the tables in the back, she walked in that direction. I smiled and said, *"Ciao, Annalisa,"* but the school intercom crackled, drowning out my voice.

> *Attention students . . . Please mark your calendars . . . The annual pep rally is scheduled for Friday, October twenty-fourth . . . The varsity soccer team will play its final regular season game at Summit the next day . . . The pep rally will begin at eight p.m., in the school parking lot . . .*

Years ago, when Millburn football was king, the pep rally was held the night before the traditional Thanksgiving Day game against Madison. My dad took me once. I remembered the walk from the St. Rose of Lima Church parking lot, as I sat on his shoulders, his large hands tight on my ankles, holding me securely against the back of his head. So many people surrounded us, talking and laughing. We continued with them along Millburn Avenue, then down the high school driveway past the gymnasium.

My dad pointed. "Jonny, that's where we're going."

Excitement welled up inside me. Packed with more people than I'd ever seen in my life, the Millburn High football grandstand was alive with movement, and the white lines on the velvet green field seemed to glow under the massive stadium lights.

"Hurry, hurry," I said. "I don't wanna miss anything."

"We'll be there soon enough," my dad assured me.

The rest of the night was spectacular. The football players stood at the edge of the stage, while cheerleaders performed their dance routines silhouetted against an immense bonfire. The head coach gave a rousing speech, and the team captains addressed the fans, and the cheering seemed to go on all night.

It was the last time I was at a pep rally, the last time I was entranced by a bonfire, the last time I felt comfortable around so many people. Not long after, the Millburn football program became a shell of what it once was. Victories dropped from double digits to half that, and in some seasons even less. Then one year some idiot tossed a brick of firecrackers into the bonfire. The explosive *rat-a-tat-tat* scared children and pissed off enough parents that the board of education stepped in to cancel the pep rally indefinitely. And so, the Wednesday night before the Thanksgiving Day game against Madison became just a night before a holiday.

But, a few years ago, Millburn's newly appointed athletic director, Mr. Meiers, began a campaign to resurrect the tradition. He had been looking for a way to celebrate the town's athletic teams. Football was a past glory, and people in town certainly weren't going to gather on a chilly October evening to cheer on the field hockey or cross country teams. The present was soccer; the future was this prodigy in town—Kyle Saint-Claire. So the pep rally was reinstated for the Friday night before the soccer team's regular season finale against archrival Summit.

Even in its new incarnation, I never had a good reason to go to the pep rally. I wondered if I would this year.

I felt a thump on my shoulder. Kyle dropped his books on the table and sat down opposite me.

"We herd from one classroom to the next like mindless cattle," he said. "Day in and day out. Everyone's the same. No one acts differently, talks differently, or thinks differently."

"What'd someone scuff your cleats?" I said.

"Don't be a wiseass," he said. "How're those problems coming?"

"Working on them."

"Need help?"

"I'll get them done," I said.

"Suit yourself."

I noticed Stephanie at the cafeteria entrance. She saw Kyle and made a beeline to our table. "I need the keys to your car," she said in a hurry.

"What for?" Kyle said.

"I, uh, left a notebook on the back seat this morning," she said.

"Go get 'em yourself," Kyle said. Stephanie held out her hand. On it, he wrote three numbers. "The keys are in my hall locker. Don't let anyone see this."

"Yeah, sure," Stephanie said. "I promise not to write this on the girls' bathroom wall."

"I'm serious," Kyle said. "Don't forget to lock the car. And bring the keys back."

"*Ciao*, little boys," Stephanie said, leaving with a flourish, before heading toward Annalisa.

"Did you hear the announcement?" I said to Kyle.

"About what?"

"The pep rally?"

He gave me a look. "Why in the world would I give a crap about the pep rally?"

I smirked. "The captain's speech."

"Captain's speech?"

"You're the captain this year," I said. "You give the speech."

"Sorry, not interested," Kyle said. "Maybe I'll let Pete or Solomon do it. Better yet, I'll make Maako do it."

"Sure you want that? People are going to this thing to see and hear *you*. There'll be newspaper reporters, I'll bet. Cable TV cameras, probably. Besides, Maako'll probably screw it up."

"Might make the whole thing worth watching."

I shrugged. "Fine, give Maako the spotlight. He deserves it."

The idea suddenly didn't seem to sit well with Kyle. "Tell you what, I'll make you get up there," he said.

"Me?"

"Yeah."

"Oh, I'd give a speech," I said. "I'd give a killer speech. Scare up some of the town's skeletons from out of the closet. Definitely none of that rah-rah crap. People see only the surface. They need to know what's going on underneath. Give me the chance. I'd deliver a speech this town'd remember a long, long time."

Kyle rolled his eyes. "Yeah, that's all we need." He picked up his books. "Pennyweather's got video from New Providence's last game. I'm gonna watch it in his office. Work on those problems."

He started to walk away, then stopped. He leaned over and nodded to where Annalisa had been sitting. "I saw you checking her out," he said. "Remember: Look, but don't touch."

THE MILLBURN TEAM SHUFFLED into the locker room. Guys wiped the sweat off their faces and raked the muddy grass from their cleats. There wasn't any talk; there wasn't much to say. Whether it was the humidity or the sloppy conditions, we had played the first half more like the worst team in the conference than the best.

Maako punched a locker. "We're losin' one to nothing to New Providence. *New Providence,* for Christ's sake. How 'bout our offense playin' some damn offense?"

Richie shook his head. "We hear you loud and clear, Maako."

"Do ya? You guys are like girls out there, afraid to get a little dirt on your uniforms."

"Drop dead," Richie snapped.

"Worry about yourself, Maako," Pete said.

Maako turned to Solomon. "How many times are ya gonna lose the ball in our end?"

"Yeah, blame me," Solomon said. "That's the answer."

"Why not? You're playin' like shit."

"How about you stop pushing forward so much?" Solomon said. Then he whipped a plastic water bottle across the room, where it exploded against the wall, just over Maako's head.

Maako didn't flinch. "I'll do what I gotta do."

Pennyweather walked into the locker room. Everyone turned to face him. Pennyweather calmly wrote on his clipboard but said nothing. He stood there for ten seconds . . .

A half minute . . .

A minute . . .

The silence turned uncomfortable . . .

Then entirely odd . . .

Finally, Pennyweather took a deep breath and spoke. "You can blame the weather, you can blame the field, you can point fingers at each other. But if you guys don't find a way to get your act together for the next thirty minutes, you'll piss away the season. Simple as that. Piss it away."

Then he walked out.

That was it? That was the best Pennyweather could offer? Maybe the heat and humidity had gotten to *him*. The players looked around, bewildered. An inferior opponent was beating us, and our coach apparently had no clue how to fix it. The team was on its own. One of us had to step forward and grab the reins.

Something compelled me to stand up. I knew what to say. I knew how to say it. I had thought about game situations like this a thousand times. I understood New Providence's modified triple-team on Kyle was forcing play to the outside of the field, where the grass was the slickest and our wingers, Gallo and Richie, couldn't get any traction. I recognized that any time we penetrated New Providence's zone, they would drop two or three offensive players back on defense, allowing their sweeper the freedom to attack the ball.

I had read about the soccer greats and what each had done in similar situations to snatch victory from defeat. I could tell the team about Portugal's Eusebio and how he single-handedly overcame a three-goal deficit in a 1966 World Cup quarterfinal match by scoring four goals of his own. Maybe that would rally the team. I glanced around the room.

The players were waiting for a leader; they needed a leader. I felt my legs tighten and my stomach flutter. This could be *my* moment. But I hesitated. Who was I? No one would listen to me. Maako would probably laugh me out of the room. I was just a backup, a scrub; how in the world could I know what to say? I didn't score enough goals or assists. What gave me the right—

Kyle stood up.

"Maako, play your damn position. And no more of your blame-everyone-else crap," he said. "Pete, Gallo, and Richie, spread out to open passing lanes up front, but try to keep the ball to the middle of the field. I'm gonna push forward. Brad, play more defense, in case I get beat."

Kyle started toward the locker room door. Quietly, the team followed him out onto the field.

▢▢▢▢

Momentum turned early in the third quarter. Richie stole the ball from a New Providence defender and immediately fed Gallo, cutting into the box, who flicked a shot past the goalie.

Yet that was all the offense our team could muster and, as time ticked away in the fourth, the game seemed destined to end in a tie. For New Providence, that was as good as a victory. For us, it would be devastating. Three weeks in, and our quest for a perfect season would be over.

"Let's go, Kyle!" Mr. Saint-Claire shouted from the stands. "It's time!"

The ball rolled out-of-bounds in front of the New Providence bench. Kyle brushed the sweat off his brow. Maybe he heard his father. Or maybe he simply knew if Millburn was going to win, it was now or never. His expression turned. It had taken nearly the entire game, but I finally saw that look on his face—the look that told me, when the game was on the line, Kyle Saint-Claire did not falter.

Receiving the throw-in from Maynard just off the center circle, Kyle started down the right side. Richie moved to the inside, drawing the attention of the weary New Providence defenders. Space opened up. Kyle pushed the ball ahead, using his speed to outrun opposing midfielders scrambling back to stop him.

"Push up, push up!" Pennyweather shouted to our back line.

Kyle faked a through pass to Richie, then stepped on top of the ball, leaving it motionless in the slick grass. A New Providence player slid past him. More opponents overpursued. Kyle dribbled to the top of the penalty area, splitting the last two defenders. The New Providence goalkeeper stepped up to cut down Kyle's angle, then crouched. Kyle planted his right foot and swept his left cleat through. Perfect. The ball sailed into the upper corner of the net, beyond the diving goalkeeper.

The Millburn fans erupted. Guys on the bench jumped to their feet. Pennyweather pumped his fist. Kyle loped around with his arms held high, his face beaming.

On the other side of the field, the New Providence players hung their heads. They had given a valiant effort, but it was all for nothing. In the immediate aftermath of

Kyle's remarkable goal, what I remembered most was the look of defeat on the goalkeeper's face as he slumped forward on his knees—a look that quickly became a nod of admiration.

A minute and a half later, the referee blew the whistle to end the game.

TWO OUTS, NOBODY ON, the Yankees leading by three runs . . . Now batting for Baltimore in the bottom of the seventh . . ."

I leaned back on my pillow. The bedroom lights were off and the radio was on, but I was hardly listening. Instead, I was remembering Kyle's goal, running it through in my mind, trying to comprehend how he had been able to keep his composure at such a critical moment in the game. I wondered if he blocked out the pressure, or whether the pressure was what helped him raise his skills even higher than they already were. I hoped I could do the same if I was ever in that situation. But I wasn't sure.

"And the pitch . . . There's a fly ball to shallow center-field . . ."

Through my open window, I noticed the sound of a soccer ball being kicked. I glanced at the clock. It was almost ten thirty. Curious, I walked over to the window.

The Saint-Claires' house was lit up like a Christmas tree. Lights were on in every room, and Kyle's car was parked at an angle in the driveway so that the headlights shined on the lawn.

Mr. Saint-Claire stood at their front door. "Give this a half hour more before you turn in for the night," I heard him say.

Kyle waited until his father went inside; then he flicked the ball in the air. Right foot—left foot—right foot—right foot—left foot—left knee—right knee—left knee—left knee—left foot—left foot—left foot—right foot—left foot—left knee—right knee—head—head—head—right foot . . .

The ball went from his cleats to his knees to his head, back and forth, left and right, yet Kyle remained in the same spot on the lawn. It was his typical display of control. He kept the ball in the air for a minute . . .

Five minutes . . .

Ten . . .

For the briefest of moments, I considered going down to the basement to lift some weights. A few sets of benches, or maybe some squats. But what was the point? Today's game left me tired; the season already had me drained. With all the pressure on Kyle, he should have been even more so.

It annoyed me that he wasn't.

AN INDIAN SUMMER HAD FINALLY given way to fall. Leaves of red, orange, and yellow swirled about the school patio. I sat alone at a table, the midday sun doing its best to warm my back, while I tried to come up with an answer for a college essay I was working on: "Describe the most significant event or moment of your life." A blank notebook page was staring back at me.

Could I really explain to some strangers that the most significant moment of my life was when an anonymous classmate created the ladder, or when the Saint-Claires moved in across the street, or the last time I threw a baseball with my dad, or the moment before I hung up the phone with Ruby's mother?

So many stellar choices.

One thing I was sure of, my moment certainly hadn't happened on a soccer field. My stats for the season were awful: seven shots, two assists, zero goals, averaging twelve minutes a game. I kept track, but I was wondering if it was worth the effort. I pushed the notebook aside. My fortunes had to get better.

A moment later, it seemed they had.

Annalisa came out of the cafeteria, alone. She looked around the patio, but because every table was taken, she walked straight toward the wall. As she passed by me, she said, "*Buongiorno,* Jonathan. Good luck for your *fútbol* match tomorrow."

"*Grazie mille,* Annalisa," I said.

That drew a smile.

She sat down on the wall, pulled a can of Diet Coke from her handbag, and opened a bag of potato chips. I watched her sip the soda through a straw, then take delicate bites from a chip. Soon, she took out a journal and started writing, then tore off a page, folded it twice, and slipped it under her leg. Pretending to work on my essay, I watched her the entire time.

Occasionally she'd look up.

And I'd smile.

It was the same game we played when we passed each other in the hallways. I figured foreign girls would be impetuous and mercurial, but Annalisa seemed nothing like that. She was shy and quiet, and if I had to guess, I would've figured she'd finish her years at Millburn High without much notice at all. Maybe that was why she became friends with Trinity and Stephanie right from the start, to ensure that she wouldn't remain on the outside looking in. In spite of this, I knew there was a lot more to Annalisa, but any time I tried to talk to her, Trinity and Stephanie would get in the way.

A few minutes later, I was sure I caught her staring at me. I considered going over and sitting next to her—screw the bet with Kyle—but getting close to Annalisa, just like a header in soccer, was all about timing. I had hesitated. When I did, the side doors burst open and Trinity and Stephanie stumbled out of the school, howling in laughter.

"Think he knows it was us?" Stephanie asked.

Trinity rolled her eyes. "Who cares? He's such a creep."

When Trinity and Stephanie saw me looking at them, they stopped talking. I figured they meant Mr. Zoffinger. He was a thin, straight-laced man who taught sophomore American history. I liked him as a teacher. There were rumors that he'd been seen making out with one of his students—not that it was the first time a male teacher had been played by a flirty sophomore. The girl in question was still unnamed, but the story seemed to be sticking. Someone was even leaving notes around the school mocking his "technique." I'd heard he might be fired.

Trinity and Stephanie ran up the patio steps and sat

on the wall beside Annalisa. Trinity grabbed the Diet Coke, while Stephanie helped herself to a handful of potato chips.

"Gives a ten-page paper due in three weeks," Trinity said, annoyed. "We're gonna have to get that changed pronto." She took a gulp, then winced. "What the hell—is this just soda?"

"It is," Annalisa said, sheepishly. "I am sorry."

Trinity tossed the can away, then pulled a pack of cigarettes from her pocket and smacked it against her hand— empty. "I need a smoke real bad. I thought I was gonna lose it in class."

"Let's go downtown," Stephanie said.

"Got some cash?" Trinity said.

"No."

"Then we'll hit the deli," Trinity said. "Whose turn to distract the cashier?"

"I did it last time," Stephanie said.

"Then I'm up," Trinity said. She turned to Annalisa. "And you're gonna help."

Annalisa looked confused. *"Che?"*

"Don't worry," Stephanie said. "I won't let anything happen to you."

"But we have *biologia*," Annalisa said. "Uh, I mean, biology."

Trinity swung her legs off the back of the patio wall and jumped down. "You're in America, Annalisa," she said, grabbing her by the arm. "Didn't you ever ditch class back home?"

Before she could answer, Trinity pulled her along. I noticed Annalisa left the piece of paper on the wall. After the three girls were gone, I walked over, picked up the paper, and unfolded it. In loops and curls, Annalisa had written her name and a phone number. I quickly slipped it in my jacket pocket.

SHOOT IT, JONNY!" SOMEONE YELLED.

It could have been a teammate, or Pennyweather, or one of the hundreds of Millburn fans standing on our sideline. Seven minutes into our home game against Dayton—after our left winger, Gallo, had been helped off the field with a sprained knee—and the only thing between me and the opposing goalkeeper was the ball and God's green earth.

The situation was severely unexpected.

Moments before, Solomon had headed a corner kick out of our defensive zone. When a Dayton player misplayed the clear, Maako stole the ball and took off downfield. He should've passed the ball to Kyle or to one of our outside midfielders. It was what everyone expected. But Maako didn't. Instead, he called a switch with our stopper, dribbled past two Dayton midfielders, and sprinted toward the goal.

I filled the space between the Dayton center and left fullback. On the slim chance that Maako would fake a pass to Kyle on his left, I'd be open on his right just inside the penalty area. And that's exactly what happened. Maako delivered a short cross.

I trapped the ball off my chest. Then all hell broke loose. I don't know if I was breathing, though I must have been because I remember hearing air whoosh in and out of my mouth. I could feel the energy drain from my body. Another few strides and I'd crash.

Footsteps to my left.

Footsteps to my right.

Footsteps at my heels.

The Dayton goalkeeper charged. I reached my leg back and crushed the ball, just as the goalkeeper slid, flipping me into the air. For a split second I thought about how cool this must've looked: Backup striker subs in for starting left winger, makes a strong move inside the box, gives up his body in a fierce collision, puts the home team ahead, 1–0. I hit the ground hard, and whipped my head around just in time to see my masterpiece.

Instead, I watched the ball sail over the crossbar. There was a loud groan from our sideline. Pennyweather, fists at his hips, his face rigid, said nothing. I got to my feet and quickly set up to play defense.

Maako ran by. "Get on top of the damn ball, Fehey!"

By the start of the third quarter, Gallo returned to the field and I was back on the bench, where I remained for the rest of the game. It gave me plenty of time to think about how the margin between glory and continued anonymity was razor thin. I didn't control my nerves when I received Maako's pass. I rushed the execution. What had all the training with Kyle been for if I couldn't handle the pressure against a mediocre team like Dayton? I didn't relax. I didn't keep my head. I should've leaned over the ball more. But I didn't. Because of that, I put a sliver of lift into the shot, sending the ball into, what was for all intents and purposes, oblivion.

□□□□

Kyle pulled the BMW up his driveway and parked. "Good win today," he said as we got out of the car.

"Sure." I started toward my house. "Your goals were nice," I said, more out of obligation than really meaning it.

The final score was 4–0. A shutout victory. That should have been the important part. Winning—that's all that mattered, right? Millburn soccer drew the crowds it did because it won games. Plain and simple. Winning put you on a pedestal; losers looked up from below. Winners were afforded the spoils of victory; losers got nothing.

But there was more to it than that. What did it mean to be on a winning team if you weren't a starter or at least playing a lot? I thought about that all the time. I'm sure every backup did. Team glory wasn't worth much if you were rarely in the battle. "You're riding the starters' coattails," people would say behind your back. Or to your face. It was about a million times worse if you were that second-stringer who did get a chance to be in the battle, but air-mailed a golden opportunity to score over the crossbar.

Kyle said something.

I turned. "What?"

"And an assist," he said. "Two goals *and* an assist. I got the assist on the last goal. College coaches like to see stuff like that. They wanna know if you're a team player and all."

"Yeah, okay," I said.

□ □ □ □

My mom sat in her chair in the corner of our living room. A lamp shined on the book she was reading. To the side of the chair was a wineglass. She looked up. "How'd it go?"

"We won," I said. Halfheartedly, I guess.

"That's a good thing, right?"

I didn't answer. I had my uniform in my hands.

"Leave them in the laundry room," my mom said. "I warmed up some food for you."

I put the clothes on top of the washing machine, then took a chicken pot pie from the oven and sat down at the kitchen table. I pierced the crust with a fork. Steam rose from the inside.

Why did Maako pass me the ball? The one guy on the team I truly despised, a loudmouthed egotistical jerkoff, and he delivers a pass to me when I would've bet my life he wouldn't. And a goddamn perfect pass, too.

Maybe if I had cushioned the ball with my chest differently . . . My body suddenly—almost involuntarily— twisted to a better angle, and I felt that familiar rush of nervousness, as if the soccer ball were coming at me at that instant. Then I just felt stupid. The game was long over. My screwup was long over. I took a bite, then sat back from the table and shut my eyes.

THE LIBRARY WAS QUIET. It always was. It kind of reminded me of the attic.

I had spent the past few hours reading *The Great Gatsby* for an English term paper. Critiquing Fitzgerald was an impossibility. I could hardly understand his dense writing. I almost felt stupid reading the novel, and I certainly didn't care much about Manhattan or Long Island, or anything that happened way back in the 1920s. But I liked Gatsby. He was a mystery. People wanted to know him. They wanted to be around him. They wanted to be with him. And he had money. A ton of it. Would've fit in well in Short Hills. What I didn't get was why, when the façade of his life was peeled away, Gatsby—rich, manly, and seemingly flourishing—was on the outside looking in.

I closed the novel and stared at the second floor. I hadn't bothered to go up there today. In fact, it had been weeks since the last time. I was tired of thumbing through books, tired of not finding a scrap of paper that even remotely looked like the ladder, tired of the ridiculous quest. Soccer season was taking its toll, and with senior year already well into October, maybe it wasn't worth the effort to find the ladder anyway.

Who was I kidding?

I'd be back. Next Sunday afternoon, probably. If not, definitely the one after. There were more stacks to go through. There'd always be more.

I stood up from the table and put on my jacket. Annalisa, standing at the reference desk, caught my attention. The emerald sweater she wore seemed to shine from across the drab library. I looked around to see if she was alone. I didn't see Trinity or Stephanie, or anyone else.

A librarian directed Annalisa to a corner of the library. I waited. My heart thumped as I watched her wind her way through the maze of book stacks. Maybe this was one of those moments, full of possibility, like when I sat on my dad's shoulders gazing out at the Millburn football pep rally. Or the night in Vail when Ruby straddled my legs, touched her lips to my ear, and whispered she wanted to be with me.

I picked up *Gatsby* and my notebook, walked past the second floor staircase, across an aisle, then another, and headed toward Annalisa. She was searching a book stack. But instead of tapping her on the shoulder, I veered off down the opposite aisle.

No guts, I scolded myself.

And, for some reason, that stopped me from simply walking away. Through the shelves, I could see her. I moved closer. When we were both at eye level, I coughed. She didn't notice me, so I coughed again. Then she looked at me through the shelf and said coolly, "Yes?"

"*Ciao,* Annalisa."

I ducked my head to see her face, but she moved out of view. Then I stepped around the end of the stacks. "What're you working on?"

Annalisa didn't look at me. "I am researching for class," she said. "And you? I did not know you were here."

I pointed to the other side of the library. "I was over there."

"Were you searching for something?"

"Not today," I said.

"So you did not find what you wanted?"

I hinted a smile. "Maybe now I have."

"Or maybe you need to keep looking," she said.

Annalisa moved to the other side of the stacks. I followed her.

"Gonna be done soon?" I asked.

"Why do you want to know, Jonathan?"

"We could get ice cream or something."

She shrugged. "I must do this work."

It was clear that Annalisa didn't have any interest in speaking to me. My heart sank. Trinity and Stephanie had gotten to her. I didn't think they had been able to, but I was wrong. I started to walk away.

"Why did you not telephone me?" Annalisa asked.

I stopped.

"Did you not get the notepaper I left?" she said.

"I did. I got it."

"But you did not telephone?"

"I meant to."

"Meant to?"

"Yeah."

"You should have telephoned."

I noticed Annalisa look over my shoulder. I turned. A woman had walked in the library entrance. Annalisa immediately picked up her notebooks and pen. "I must go," she said. "*Mia madre* is here."

"I'll call you," I said, louder than I wanted. "Promise."

But Annalisa did not look back.

I STOOD AT MY BEDROOM WINDOW, staring out at the Saint-Claires' house. "Come on . . . come on," I muttered. "What's taking so long?"

It felt odd being home so early after school. I expected to be exhausted, sweaty, and dirty, but was none of those. Pennyweather had finally given the team a day off. It was deserved. We were 10–0, ranked sixth in New Jersey. Yesterday, at Oradell, our midfielders turned what should have been a competitive game against a good opponent into a 7–1 shellacking.

And while Kyle reached yet another milestone—setting a school record with the fifty-first and fifty-second goals of his career—I scored on a left-footed blast off a pass from Richie in the fourth quarter. It was my first of the season, and a long time coming. I had almost forgotten what it was like to see the ball come off my foot and smack the back netting of an opponent's goal. That instantaneous release of emotion. Teammates mobbing me. Fans calling out my name. A pat on the back from Pennyweather. Damn, it had been incredible.

Kyle finally came out of his front door. I leaned back from the window to stay hidden (though surely he couldn't have seen me) as he jogged down the walkway and jumped into his BMW. He backed out of the driveway in a rush, then turned up Lake Road.

On the ride home from school, I had asked him what he was doing for the afternoon. He told me he was going to take it easy.

"Take it easy?" I said.

"Yeah, just hang out," he said.

That was b.s. People in the crowd were meeting at Brandy Stahl's house after school; more would show up later. Her parents were away. There'd be alcohol, pot, and whatever else. I knew Kyle couldn't resist.

"We got tough games coming up," he said. "I wanna be ready."

"Good idea," I said.

If Kyle wanted to have secrets, I could have secrets, too. I threw on a long-sleeved shirt and a sweatshirt, bolted out the front door, then ran down Lake Road.

As I came to South Pond, I saw Annalisa sitting patiently on the dock. She waved and gave me a delicious smile, and, suddenly, I didn't give a damn where Kyle was, who he was with, or what the hell he was doing.

For the past few weeks, Annalisa and I had been talking on the phone nearly every night. Sometimes just to say that we'd see each other in the hallway the next day, if we could. I wanted to see her a lot more, but we had to be cool about things. She had a locker near the science labs and, though I wasn't taking biology or chemistry, I found every opportunity to wander that way between periods.

On Sundays, when we weren't meeting at the library, we'd spend the afternoon on the dock at South Pond. Away from the crowd. Away from prying eyes and whispers. Just me and her. Talking, and joking, and teasing. We hadn't fooled around. Not even a kiss. There'd be time for that. Maybe it didn't need to get to that point anyway. I knew Annalisa liked getting out from Trinity and Stephanie's shadow, while I relished the idea that we had this thing together that nobody knew about.

"Where do they think you are?" I asked.

"Out shopping for winter fashion," she said.

"I'm surprised they didn't wanna go."

"They did."

Annalisa was so unlike Trinity and Stephanie. I'd wondered why the two of them bothered making her a part of their little triumvirate, since they seemed to be following in the footsteps of Sloan Ruehl. Annalisa would surely just get in the way.

"Better hope they don't find out the truth," I said.

"Yes, I do not want them mad at me. Stephanie, especially."

"You mean Trinity."

Annalisa shook her head and, for a moment, seemed serious. "No," she said. "I mean Stephanie."

"Yeah, well, she's got a big ego to fill being Kyle's little sister," I said. "I'm sure she's enjoying that."

"I do not think so," Annalisa said.

"Trust me," I said. "I've known her a long time."

But Annalisa was insistent. "Stephanie comes over my house, even without Trinity. We sit for hours in my bedroom; sometimes she stays for the night. She talks about her parents. And Kyle. Once she told me that she thought her dad wished she had been another boy—or a girl that played sports the best. She was being honest, I am sure. Sometimes we look at magazines of movie stars. I think she wants people to notice her, too." Annalisa bowed her head a little. "I guess some people like that."

"Can we talk about something else?" I asked.

Annalisa nodded.

"I'm kind of tired of all things Saint-Claire."

"But understand, Jonny, Stephanie has been good to me," Annalisa said, in earnest. "From the beginning, she told me to stay close with her and school would be fine. It was difficult coming from far away. Living in a new country, new people . . . new everything. I was worried I would not make friends in America. Stephanie fixed that."

And then we were both quiet for a moment.

As we dangled our feet just above the water's surface, I looked at Annalisa, studying her face. She was delicate, beautiful, and had flawless skin that, even with summer long over, seemed tanned. She had brought a bag of *cioccolata* and a book of poetry. We ate the candy and took turns reading our favorite poems out loud. When a small-mouthed bass jumped, not more than a few yards away, I offered my knowledge for how to catch it. I explained lures and baited hooks, and pointed out all the ideal spots for catfish and perch. Most of the time, though, we talked about teachers and school and Short Hills. I told her that everyone thought her father was in the Mafia.

She laughed. "The Mafia?"

"Yeah," I said. "Supposedly, your family moved to Short Hills so your father could set up a money laundering operation for people back home."

"Money laundering?" she said. "What is this?"

I shrugged. I didn't know.

Annalisa shook her head. "You Americans watch too many criminal movies."

In fact, the Giannis came from Arma di Taggia, a small town on the Mediterranean coast, one hundred kilometers from San Remo. Annalisa's father was an executive at an Italian telephone company working on a project with AT&T in Bedminster. The plan was for their family to stay in Short Hills for the next year or two. However, recently she overheard her parents saying that the company might transfer her father much sooner than that. Annalisa hadn't told anyone. I wished she hadn't told me.

"That'd be lousy," I said.

"I think you are right," she said.

We sat shoulder to shoulder, watching the sun set, squinting our eyes from the reflection off the pond's surface, pressing in tight when a chilly wind rustled the treetops and rippled the water. I asked if she was cold. Annalisa nodded. So I pulled off the sweatshirt I was wearing. She was curious about the logo.

"Princeton," I said. "It's where my mom went to college."

"Will you attend there, also?"

"Doubt it."

"Why?"

"My mom's super smart; I'm just kinda smart," I said. "I'll apply, but I don't wanna get my hopes up. It's my favorite sweatshirt, though."

Annalisa slipped it on. The sweatshirt fell off her thin shoulders and hung well below her waist. It looked good on her. I told her to keep it. A small gift from me. I think she liked that.

Eventually, dusk came.

"It is beautiful here," Annalisa said softly.

"Like Arma di Taggia?"

"It is beautiful there; it is beautiful here . . ." she said. "And peaceful . . ." I looked at her. She seemed to be thinking about something more. Then, she said, "'Where the quiet-colored end of evening smiles . . .'"

"What?"

"'Where the quiet-colored end of evening smiles,'" Annalisa repeated.

"What's that from?"

"Oh, no, Jonathan," she said. "You must tell me."

"I must?"

"*Sì.*"

I tried to think of something special to say. "Okay, Ms. Gianni . . ." I said, hoping a few moments' delay would help. "You tell me what this is from." I stood up, pointed to the horizon, and said in a deep, throaty voice, as if I were on stage at the Papermill Playhouse, "Behold, the brownish afterglow marking the day's lonely movement into night, and the continued ceaseless march toward our own inevitable passing . . ." I looked at Annalisa and shrugged. "Sorry, that's all I got right now."

She clapped and smiled. "I do not know what that is from."

"It's a Jonathan Fehey original."

"You made it up?"

"I did."

"Bellissima!" she said. "You are so poetic."

"I don't think so," I said, sitting down. But it did feel nice hearing her say it.

It was getting dark, so I walked Annalisa home. We took the long way, down Lake Road, over Redemption Bridge, across Western Drive, then up Highland Avenue. At her house, I followed her up the driveway. But she stopped me, kissed me on the cheek, and said, *"Sei un amico speciale."*

"What's that mean?" I said.

But she just smiled.

I watched her go inside. Then I jogged home, thinking how that was exactly, and perfectly, the way a day off should be spent.

FLASH—

My mind went black.

Then I heard voices. I could smell grass. Or dirt, maybe. Someone was pulling me up from the field. He was wearing gloves. Our goalkeeper, Stuart, I figured.

"Man, did I nail you," he said. "You okay?"

I wasn't. I got up on one knee, but my head was ringing, and I had to fight like hell from booting right there on the field.

"What . . . happened?" I heard myself mumble.

Stuart was talking, but I couldn't make total sense of what he was saying. Something about me launching myself into the air . . . for a header . . . he came out of the goal . . .

punched the ball away . . . the impact was severe . . . that was the only thing I was sure about.

Pennyweather walked up. "Heck of a collision."

"Hadn't noticed," I managed to say.

"Why don't you sit out awhile?"

"I'm fine." I undid the laces of my cleats, and then re-tied them slowly. The few extra seconds helped to clear my rattled head a little.

"Let's go!" Maako yelled. "While we're young."

Pennyweather turned. "Relax, Erik." Then he called out, "Defense stay put. First-string offense!"

I got up and jogged to the sideline as straight as I could, while the starting forwards and midfielders took their po-sitions for a corner kick. I stood, taking in deep breaths, fists at my hips. Kyle glanced over at me.

Pennyweather blew his whistle. From the corner arc, Gallo lofted an out-swinger to an area at the top of the goal area. There was a clash of players. Maako came out of the melee with the ball, taking a few strides before clearing the ball out of the zone with a booming kick. "That's how you do it, girls!"

"Same defense," Pennyweather said. "Second-string of-fense back in." He gestured to me.

"I'm okay," I said.

I half jogged back on the field and set up even with the far post of the goal area, just a few yards behind Maako, who stood at the center of the defensive zone. My vision still shimmered when my eyes were open, but I noticed no one was marking me. Willie, our backup right winger, placed the ball on the corner arc. When he looked up, I touched my finger to my hand and pointed to the near side of the goal area. Willie stepped back, then kicked the ball.

I was already running parallel to the goal line, pushing past Maako, catching enough of his thigh to knock him off his feet. Willie's corner kick was perfect, sailing head-high off the ground. I jumped up and flicked the ball with my forehead. When I looked back, I saw Stuart standing in the same spot—he hadn't even had time to react—with the ball in the back of the net. My ringing head suddenly didn't seem so bad.

There was a loud "Whoa!" from the other players.

"Hell, yeah!" someone yelled.

A few guys started clapping.

I jogged over to Willie, high-fived him; then both of us went to the sideline with the rest of the second-stringers. I looked back again. Maako was picking himself up off the ground. Little on a soccer field had ever felt sweeter.

"What the hell was that?" Maako shouted, throwing his arms in the air.

"Next group," Pennyweather called out. "Starting offense and second-string defense on the field."

Maako started toward me. "That's bullshit, Fehey."

"Enough," Pennyweather said.

But Maako ignored him. His hands were curled into fists. He started toward me, then suddenly charged, catching me by surprise. I backpedaled, but before Maako got to me, Kyle grabbed him in a bear hug. In an instant, we were surrounded by a mob of players.

"Get your hands off me!" Maako yelled at Kyle.

"Give it up," Kyle said.

"Protecting your little girlfriend?" Maako sneered.

"You're a dick, Maako," I said. I pushed forward, driving my legs into the turf, trying to get close enough to throw a punch. But I couldn't. Gallo and Maynard had ahold of me—a really good hold. They wouldn't let me move. In a voice only loud enough for me to hear, Gallo said, "Don't even think about it, Jonny."

"I'm gonna wreck you, Fehey," Maako shouted.

I laughed at him. "Sit your ass on the bench."

"The day I spend a minute on the bench with you is the day I quit this team," Maako said, then punctuated it with a wad of phlegm that whizzed past my head.

"Dirtbag," I yelled.

But Maako just grinned.

Pennyweather wedged himself into the fray. "Cut it out, you two. Start acting like men."

I thought we were.

There was still some pushing and shoving, but Pennyweather's threat to have the team run laps for the rest of practice got the other players' attention. Everyone soon calmed down. Except me and Maako. We were left to seethe on our own, spending the rest of practice doing pushups and sit-ups at opposite end lines. I didn't care. It gave my head a long time to clear.

▢▢▢▢

I knocked on the office door. "You wanted to see me?"

Pennyweather waved me in. "Take a look at this." He was watching video footage of our last game against Verona, a 3–1 victory. He pointed to the screen. "Richie's open, but Dennis doesn't see him. He's not even looking. See? That's what I'm talking about—poor execution. We can't have this when we get to the postseason tournaments . . ."

While Pennyweather continued with his analysis, I glanced around the room. There were newspaper articles tacked to a corkboard and copies of *Soccer America* spread out on the desk. Then I noticed the wall behind me.

Holy shit . . . I almost said it out loud.

Pennyweather had a framed photograph of him with Pele, Franz Beckenbauer, and Giorgio Chinaglia, teammates on the New York Cosmos. Next to it were framed tickets from the 1978 NASL Championship game at Giants Stadium. Above that was a photo of Pennyweather standing shoulder to shoulder with Rick Davis and Shep Messing, two of the first great American soccer players. But the centerpiece of the office was a ball autographed by French immortal Michel Platini, and Paolo Rossi, striker on Italy's 1982 World Cup championship team.

"Know who they all are?" Pennyweather asked.

"Of course," I said. I had read about each one. I rattled off the significance of each player. Pennyweather seemed impressed. Or, at least, surprised.

"I've been around soccer a long time," he said.

"Ever meet Mario Kempes?" I asked.

"El Matador."

"Yes."

"Nope, never did," he said.

Pennyweather turned the video off and sat down behind his desk. "Jonny, we're coming down to the wire. Only two regular season games left. Madison next Wednesday, Summit the Saturday after. Then the postseason tournaments. I don't want any unnecessary injuries in practice—the team can't afford it. And I definitely don't want injuries because of some stupid grudge."

I knew what Pennyweather was getting at. He had to coddle the starters, even someone like Maako. "I was just practicing hard," I said. "Exactly what you ask for every day."

"Practice hard, practice fair," Pennyweather said. "But no cheap shots out there."

"I never do."

"And no more fights."

"I'll try."

"Not 'try,'" he said. "No. More. Fights."

"Yes," I answered.

I wondered if there was even a snowball's chance in hell that Pennyweather would be bringing Maako into this office to read him the riot act. I wondered if Maako was entitled to more screwups than the rest of us.

"But don't back down, either," Pennyweather said, as I started out the door.

I looked back at him.

But Pennyweather was already shuffling through some papers. He didn't acknowledge that I was leaving, and I didn't say another word. It was as close as we'd ever come to some kind of understanding.

THE DOORBELL RANG. I looked at the kitchen clock. It was ten thirty—late for anyone to be stopping by, even for a Saturday night. I walked into the front hallway, called out to my mom, "I got it," and opened the door.

It was the last person I would have expected. Trinity, with raccoon eyes and a pretentious pout, was leaning oh-so-casually against one of the portico columns, wearing knee-high boots buckled from top to bottom, a black skirt, and fishnet top. Her Celtic knot and purple fingernails glinted in the dim light.

"Hello, Jonny-boy," she said.

Out of the darkness, Stephanie stepped up, too. The similarity was startling. Her hair was the same jet-black color as Trinity's, her makeup just as bold. She wore a black coat over black plastic pants, and a metal choker around her neck.

"What do you want?" I said. "I've got a mac and cheese in the oven."

"Tsk . . . tsk," Trinity said. "Two hotties on your front porch and all you can think about is food?"

"That is a shame," Stephanie said.

"Silly little sophomore girls . . ." I shook my head. "I gotta go."

"Worried we silly little sophomore girls might be too much for you to handle?" Trinity said.

"Are we 'untouchable'?" Stephanie said. The girls looked at each other and giggled. "Kyle's out. Why aren't you, Jonny-boy?"

"I'm busy."

"Wankin' it?"

"You enjoy being a wench?" I said.

"Wench?" Stephanie said. "That's a bit dated, don't-cha think?"

"How about 'bitch'?"

"Now, now," Trinity said, "no more name-calling. Let's just cut to the chase. We need something from you, Jonny-boy."

I laughed. "And why in the world would I wanna give you two *anything?*"

Trinity smirked. She crossed her arms so that her breasts pressed together and lifted high, while the neckline of her top slipped down. Stephanie unbuttoned her coat, revealing a black lace bra that seemed at least a size too small. I thought I saw the edge of her nipple.

I looked back inside the house to make sure my mom wasn't coming down the stairs, then closed the door behind me. I'd let Trinity and Stephanie take things as far as they wanted. Why not? They weren't ordinary sophomores; everyone at school already knew that. Girls in their grade stayed away from them. Most juniors did, too. They had already served a day of detention for knocking the snot out of a girl who teased Annalisa in the gym bathroom. Mr. Zoffinger was only the most recent target of their cruel intentions.

"Like what ya see?" Trinity said.

"Nothing special," I said.

"Maybe if I . . ." Stephanie said, leaning over and pretending to brush something off her shoes, her eyes fixed on mine. Slowly, she stood up. "Or maybe, if this slipped a little." She ran her thumb under a bra strap, sliding it off her shoulder. "Want some more?"

I shrugged, trying to seem as disinterested as possible.

Trinity laughed. "Ha, I'll bet you do, Jonny-boy. Gotta little rise out of you, didn't we?" She put her hand on my crotch with a practiced touch. "There's more where that came from," she said, with a gentle squeeze before letting go. "First, we need to establish a little quid pro quo. You do for us; we do for you. We noticed you have an interest in our Annalisa."

"She's adorable," Stephanie said.

"With a hot body," Trinity said.

"We think she's homesick," Stephanie said.

"She needs some lovin' to distract her, Jonny-boy," Trinity said. "You can swoop right in and make her a very happy Italian girl. Of course, as you know, there are plenty of guys at school who've noticed her, too."

I wanted so badly to laugh in Trinity's face and tell her I talked to Annalisa all the time—practically every night— and that we hung out together at South Pond, and at the library, and had private moments at school whenever we could. Best of all, that I knew things about her that the two of them would never know.

"Get to the point, *Beverly*," I said.

Trinity did her best to smile, but I knew I'd pissed her off. "See, Jonny-boy, we wanna go to a party at the circle. Now, we know your rep's not too good. You're not that high on the—" She turned to Stephanie. "What's it called again?"

"The ladder," Stephanie said.

"Yes, the ladder," Trinity said. "You're not high enough on the ladder to go to the circle yourself."

"You're wasting my time," I said.

"Hey, don't kill the messenger," Trinity said. "It is what it is."

"Why the circle?" I asked.

"Where you been, Jonny-boy?" Trinity said. "All the coolest older guys go to parties at the circle. It's *the* place to be. I bet it's the place you wanna be, too. Now, we heard some senior girls talking about hanging out there the night of the county championship game. Win or lose, it's gonna rock."

"The key is my brother," Stephanie said.

"Kyle?" I said.

"All you gotta do is convince him," Stephanie said.

"To do what?"

"To let us go," Stephanie said. "*All* of us."

"Simple," Trinity said.

"Why me?"

"Why not?" Trinity said.

"Why *me?*" I repeated.

Stephanie feigned a sigh. "Because you wanna go as bad as we do. And Kyle might say yes to you. You want it; we want it. Everyone'll be happy."

I leaned back against the front door.

"Jonny, we know you're not a loser," Trinity said in a syrupy-sweet voice. "If you get us to a party at the circle, this won't be the only time we get to"—she pretended to search for the right words—"share an experience like this. And you won't have to stay home all by your lonesome self." She giggled. "Well, at least for one night."

Inside, the oven buzzer went off.

"Now run along to your mac and cheese," Trinity said. "We've got plans to make."

The two girls were down the front walkway and crossing Lake Road. They looked back at me, laughing and carrying on. Soon, the front door of the Saint-Claires' house opened and closed, and Trinity and Stephanie were gone.

FLAMES REACHED HIGH INTO the night's sky. On the stage behind the bonfire, Pennyweather waved to the crowd. To his left and right, the eleven starters stood, chests out, hands clasped behind their backs, pompously serious expressions on their faces. Camera flashes were going off, the school band was playing, and the varsity cheerleaders were chanting, along with the crowd, "We will, we will . . . rock you! We will, we will . . . rock you!"

Pennyweather stepped up to the microphone and pointed from one end of the line of players to the other. "This is your fifteen-and-oh undefeated varsity team, Millburn. These are your boys. I'm proud of every one of them. They're good students, good citizens, and all season long they've given every bit of their heart and soul, every ounce of their sweat and pain." He pumped his fist.

Hundreds of townspeople, young and old, roared their approval.

"It's been another successful season, so far . . . But our team needs your support for this last regular season game. And, after that, for the county and state tournaments," Pennyweather continued. "Show how important this team is to this town—our town!"

Someone cried out from the back of the crowd, "Go get 'em, Millburn!"

"Yes! Yes!" Pennyweather shouted. "That's what we need, some real emotion."

Another man bellowed, "We're gonna beat Scummit!"

"We will, we will," Pennyweather said, nodding. Someone handed him a red jersey. He held it up high. On the front, it said SUMMIT SOCCER. With great fanfare, Pennyweather wadded the jersey in a ball and tossed it in the bonfire.

The fans erupted.

"Let me introduce our lineup," Pennyweather said. "Our goalie . . . with fifteen career shutouts and an oh-point-eight goals-against average . . . Stuart Masterson." Stuart stepped forward and waved to the crowd.

The backups had gathered at the side of the stage. Pennyweather told us to meet there. Everyone on the team was equal, he assured us, but he would be able to introduce only the first-stringers. I guess some players were more equal than others. Screw that. I wasn't going to look lame standing next to the stage, staring up at the starters like they were gods.

I felt a tap on my shoulder.

"*Ciao,* Jonathan," Annalisa said.

"*Buonasera,*" I said.

She smiled and said, "This is so wonderful. I cannot believe there are all these people. Should we move up closer?"

"I can see fine from here."

Annalisa seemed to understand. She looked toward the stage again. "Yes, I think I can, too." The flames flickered in her eyes.

"So you like it?" I said.

"What?"

"The bonfire?"

She looked at me. "I do not understand."

"The fire." I pointed. "When it's big like that it's called a bonfire."

"I *do* like it," she said. "But I do not understand—why is it there?"

I wasn't sure what the connection was between our high school soccer team and a fifteen-foot-high fire, with hundreds of people standing before it like they were worshiping a pagan deity. Tradition, I guess. But there had to be more to it than that. Maybe it was human nature to be drawn to something so mesmerizing yet at the same time so dangerous.

On stage, Pennyweather was finishing the introductions. "Last, but certainly not least . . . Millburn's season and career record-holder for goals and assists. . . . an all-conference, all-county, and all-state selection each of the past two years . . . your captain . . . Kyle Saint-Claire!"

The crowd's cheer was louder than for any of the other players.

"Will you win tomorrow?" Annalisa asked.

I nodded toward the stage and said, "Yeah, I think so."

Kyle moved behind the microphone. "Tomorrow's a, uh, big game for our team. We'd like to take home the conference title again. But we need your support. We don't do it alone. We can't do it alone . . ."

Kyle went on, but with Annalisa beside me, I stopped listening. I leaned into her, smelling her perfume.

"'Love Among the Ruins' by Robert Browning," I whispered in her ear. "Where the quiet-colored end of evening smiles. Miles and miles on the solitary pastures where our sheep, half-asleep, tinkle homeward thro' the twilight."

"You remembered," Annalisa said with delight. *"Molto buono."*

"I'm still trying to figure out what it—"

"Annalisa," Trinity interrupted. She and Stephanie stepped in front of us. They both reeked of pot, and I could see a bottle of liquor hidden inside Trinity's jacket. "We were looking all over for you," she said.

"We thought you were lost," Stephanie said.

"She wasn't lost," I said.

"We thought she was," Trinity said.

"She was right here," I said.

"And that's lost." Trinity stared at me pointedly. "Now she's not."

As the two girls led her away, Annalisa called out in her sweet accent, "Good night, Jonathan!"

Before I could return the same, Trinity looked over her shoulder and motioned to the stage. "Quid pro quo, Jonny-boy."

I OPENED MY EYES and propped myself up on an elbow. When the cobwebs of sleep cleared, the nervousness came quickly.

Game day.

Away, against Summit.

Our undefeated record at stake.

The Suburban Conference title on the line.

My equipment bag sat beside my bed, packed the night before with my uniform and gear. My cleats were waiting in the garage. I needed to quell my nerves, so I lay down on the floor with my legs outstretched. I touched my knees . . . ankles . . . and toes . . . then grabbed the soles of my feet. I stretched my hamstrings and quads . . . my back and arms . . . Still, I was tight.

As the season wore on, I'd earned more playing time. In fact, during the last few games, I'd played nearly as much as some of the starters. I guess I could thank Kyle for that. All that damn training this summer was finally paying off. Today I was sure Pennyweather would sub me in a few times. His call down the bench, "Fehey!" could come at any time. I had to be ready.

I looked toward the window. It seemed cloudy. I just hoped it wasn't raining. I stood up, walked over, and pushed open the curtains.

"Oh . . . my . . . God . . ."

I wasn't sure what I was seeing.

I blinked a few times, but still wasn't sure.

The Saint-Claires' house was swathed in red-colored toilet paper. It was everywhere. Crisscrossing the roof. Hanging from branches. Draped over bushes. Scattered on the lawn. Wrapped around Kyle's BMW so much that you could hardly tell the car was black. He and his father came from the back of their house, each with armfuls of red paper. Mr. Saint-Claire tore down what he could reach, while Kyle gathered the rest on the lawn with a rake. Both were fuming, I could tell.

I thought about going outside to help, but a couple of

our neighbors had already walked over to pick up whatever they could.

Within a few minutes, a Millburn police car stopped along Lake Road. Mr. Saint-Claire spoke to the officer, shaking his head and pointing to where the toilet paper had been hanging. It seemed all the officer could offer was a sympathetic nod.

It was a stunning prank, in its target and execution. Of course, whoever had done this now had surely awakened the beast in Kyle. That wouldn't be a good thing for the Summit soccer team.

□□□□

In the cramped visitors' locker room, Pennyweather wrote SUMMIT in caps at the top of the chalkboard—the chalk chipped each time he scratched a letter—then underlined it twice. Below that, he continued:

14—1 overall record.
Ranked 10th—New Jersey.
Ranked 1st—Union County.
Ranked 2nd—Suburban Conference.

Summit was nearly our equal, and the final team that stood in our way of a perfect regular-season record and a number-one seed in the Essex County tournament. Penny-weather stepped back from the chalkboard.

"They're gonna come at us differently today," he said. "I'm expecting them to line up five midfielders." He pointed to Kyle. "Two guys will focus exclusively on you."

It was nothing new. Teams had double- and triple-teamed him all season. It might work for a half, maybe even three quarters, but eventually Kyle's speed and pursuit would wear the opposition down.

"They'll put three on their frontline and have just two defenders back," Pennyweather said. "I spoke to the Summit coach yesterday. His players thought our win against them earlier this month was a fluke. They say a couple of their starters were less than a hundred percent. They blame the loss on a virus going around school."

"That's bullshit," Maako said.

"But they _believe_ it," Pennyweather said. "And whatever they believe is their reality." He stared around the room. "Make no mistake about it; Summit thinks they can score on us. Especially here on their home field, with their fans. They think they're gonna win this game and ruin our season." He looked at Maako. "You gotta play smart today. You can't push up too far. We're gonna get burned by that. And keep your damn emotions in check.

"Guys on the bench," Pennyweather said. "Be ready to come into the game. It's been a long season. We'll need fresh legs." Pennyweather put the chalk down and brushed off his hands. "We fight for every ball in the air, every ball on the ground. Put it all on the line today." He made a point to stare directly at Kyle. "Ignore all other garbage."

With a goal in each game this year and the last nine of last season, Kyle had set a team and conference record for consecutive games scored and was just one away from the Essex County record—the fifth longest streak in state history. The *Star-Ledger* had mentioned it in an article a few days ago. When we arrived at the locker room, the article was taped to the door. Across it someone had written THE STREAK ENDS TODAY, in red ink. Kyle tore it down with a swipe of his hand.

"We can't have any letdowns, physical or mental," Pennyweather said. "Take a few minutes; then let's get out there."

After Pennyweather left, our players finished their final preparations, adjusting equipment and stretching. A seething anger filled the locker room.

"My cleats are sharpened," Maako said. "I'm cuttin' someone today. They're gonna bleed Scummit red."

"The first guy who tries to beat me down the side," Brad growled, "I'm takin' him out."

I walked over to Kyle. "You ready?"

"I'm ready," he said to me, then to nobody—or everybody—in particular, "Don't get in my way today."

He slammed his locker shut and called out to the team. "Let's whip these guys."

□□□□

Under a ceiling of gray clouds, an afternoon chill had descended on the field, while wind that swept along the Summit High School grounds shed the trees of their few remaining leaves.

On our sideline stood classmates, teachers, and administrators, players on the JV team, hundreds of people from town, and dozens of players' families. Among the crowd, I saw Annalisa with Trinity, Stephanie, and Mr. and Mrs. Saint-Claire.

"We are . . . the Millburn Millers!" our cheerleaders chanted. "We are . . . the Millburn Millers!"

The team stood in a circle around Kyle, following his lead on reps of sit-ups and pushups; then we broke off in pairs and groups of three for quick passing and trapping drills.

Summit fans crowded the home sideline, while the stands behind their bench were filled to capacity. One man—a bald, fat man in a red sweatshirt—stood out.

"The streak ends today, Saint-Claire!" he shouted in a bloated voice. There was a smattering of chuckles from the people around him.

This was nothing new. At away games, there was

usually an opposing fan or two who would yell something at Kyle. He always acted as if he didn't hear a word. This time Kyle looked over. The fat man in the red sweatshirt laughed in a loud, pathetic way, drawing more attention to himself.

"Captains," the referee called out.

Warm-ups ended.

While Kyle and the two Summit captains met at the center of the field with the referee and two linesmen, both teams—Millburn in blue, Summit in cardinal red— huddled around their coaches. I watched Kyle. He and the opposing captains shook hands. The referee flipped the coin. Summit won and chose to kick off.

"Make sure your head's in the game right from the start," Pennyweather said. "They're gonna come hard. Go hard right back at 'em. We've worked our butts off all season for a moment like this. Hands in!" We pushed in tight, each of us reaching our hands to the center. "Destiny is within our grasp. Don't let any team get in the way. Especially not Summit. On three . . . One. Two. Three."

"Let's go, Millburn!" the team shouted.

Our starting eleven sprinted to their positions on the field, while the backups took a place on the bench. The referee set the ball at the center of the circle, called out to make sure both goalkeepers were ready, then blew the whistle to begin the game.

Just as Pennyweather said, Summit pressed the attack,

sending five offensive players into our defensive zone, forcing Stuart to make one acrobatic save after another. The Summit coaches must have scouted us well, because they knew exactly how to exploit our only weakness—a lack of speed from our outside fullbacks. And unlike in our first game against them, when Kyle controlled the midfield, Summit's aggressive double-team was keeping him from getting into any rhythm. Only once in the first quarter was Kyle able to get a shot on net, which was easily scooped up by the opposing goalkeeper.

Pennyweather subbed me in at the beginning of the second quarter. I got a firsthand look at Summit's relentlessness. Their slide tackles weren't just knocking the ball away from us, but taking us out. And their elbows came up high, while they rode us off the ball with their shoulders. The referee called an endless number of fouls. It was just the kind of start-and-stop play that I was sure the Summit coaches intended.

Fortunately, Maako was dishing out as much as the rest of our team was taking. He won every battle in the air and got his foot on nearly every loose ball. Though we could've been down a goal or maybe even two, our back line was playing just well enough to bend but not break.

That was until three minutes and forty-one seconds were left in the half. After a scramble for the ball at the corner of the penalty area, one of the Summit wingers took a wild, off-balance shot that completely surprised

Stuart. The ball hit the bottom of the crossbar and spun in.

The Summit fans, led by the fat man in red, roared their approval.

□□□□

After halftime, I returned to the bench and watched as, late in the third quarter, our fortunes changed in an instant. Richie, who had been quiet the entire game, stole the ball from a Summit fullback, then slid a shot inside the goalpost. Just like that, we were back in the game, tied 1–all.

It seemed to be the spark our offense needed. Gallo hit the post a few minutes later, and soon after, Kyle blistered a shot that the Summit goalie barely deflected away with his forearm.

In the middle of the fourth, Pennyweather put me back in. I was better prepared this time. I made sure to knock or push a Summit player whenever I could. The rest of our team was doing the same. Every loose ball was a dogfight, every free kick a scuffle for position. The back-and-forth jawing between our players and theirs escalated, inciting both sidelines.

"Saint-Claire, you ain't gonna score!" the fat man in red yelled.

Kyle looked toward the man.

I didn't think a heckler could distract Kyle, but maybe I didn't know Kyle completely. I didn't understand what it was like to be the town's soccer star. I'd never had newspaper articles written about me. I was never stopped in the hallway on game day and asked by one teacher after another how I was feeling. I had no idea what it was like to be watched, examined, and pampered, all for the sake of what Kyle could do best—score goals and dominate soccer games. So, while the fat man seemed like an annoyance earlier in the game, with a few minutes left and the score still knotted at one, he had become a major pain in the ass.

The man pointed to the scoreboard. "Don't see your name up there, Saint-Claire!"

Kyle called for a pass from Maynard, receiving the ball just off the center circle, and quickly split two midfielders. As the Summit sweeper came up, Kyle stepped over the ball, then stepped over it again, leaving the sweeper to trip over his own feet.

"Ball!" I called out to Kyle.

It was the perfect deception. He faked a pass to me, jumped over a sliding defender, then struck the ball with the inside of his right cleat, curling it around the goalkeeper. I watched the flight of the ball as it grazed the outside of the goalpost. A second later, a Summit fullback slid into Kyle's legs from the opposite side, buckling his knees and dropping him to the grass.

"He wasn't going for the damn ball, ref!" I yelled.

"Watch your tone, son," the referee said.

The Summit player jogged away, smirking. Kyle got to his feet, but before the referee could step in, another Summit player bumped him with his shoulder. Kyle pushed that player to the ground. Both sidelines, already on edge, exploded with taunts and jeers. Players from both teams crowded into a mass.

Kyle's eyes were suddenly wide with rage. "He spit at me!" he yelled, pointing at one of the Summit players.

I wanted to put my fist down that guy's throat. I'd bring on some mayhem. But, as mad as I was, I knew that would be a huge mistake. I'd get a red card and be tossed from the game, leaving us a man down, then perhaps be disciplined by the conference and have to sit out the Essex County tournament. Besides, I fully expected the referee to give one, if not both, of the Summit players cards. He might not have seen the spit, but he surely couldn't have overlooked the foul. That deserved a yellow card, at least, and Millburn would be awarded a direct kick.

The referee, however, pointed to the corner of the goal area and announced, "Goal kick, Summit."

"What the hell?" Pennyweather yelled. He raced in from the sideline, stepping up close to the referee, his head jerking and spittle flying from his mouth. "Maybe you miss one, but you can't miss *two* fouls. Are we playing soccer or a goddamn football game?"

But the referee wouldn't listen. "Goal kick," he repeated, before threatening Pennyweather with an ejection.

Pennyweather got in a few choice last words, then walked off the field. Players for both teams moved into position. The Summit goalkeeper placed the ball down and the referee blew the whistle.

Play continued.

But Kyle didn't follow the flight of the ball up the Summit sideline. Instead, he was running alongside the referee.

"You blew that one," he said.

"Play on."

"Open your damn eyes, ref."

"It's my call."

"And you blew it."

A whistle screamed, stopping play. "Mr. Saint-Claire," the referee said, "I wear the stripes, I blow the whistle, I make the call." He pulled out a yellow card and held it high. Kyle reluctantly walked away.

"No crying in soccer, Saint-Clarabelle!" the fat man in red shouted. "Need some toilet paper to wipe away the tears?"

Kyle's face hardened. Something was very wrong. When play started again, he sprinted toward the ball. A Summit player ran at the ball, too. But when a ferocious collision with Kyle seemed imminent, he veered off. Kyle should have put his cleat on top of the ball, pivoted, and made a run down the sideline. He should've thought about putting Millburn ahead and keeping his scoring streak alive. But he didn't, I guess. Just as the ball neared the sideline, Kyle drilled the ball—I mean, *drilled* it—out of bounds, at an insanely close distance, way too close for the fat man to put up a hand or turn away. The impact echoed across the field. It was a sickening sound.

"No way . . ." I heard someone say.

It was me.

With less than eight minutes left in the game, fans were charging onto the field, following players from both benches. I ran straight to Kyle. So did Mr. Saint-Claire. There was swearing and cursing, and plenty of grabbing and shoving. Amid the chaos, it occurred to me how bizarre it was being out in the middle of the field, ready to throw a punch instead of playing the game.

"Scummit losers!" someone from Millburn shouted.

"See *you* after the game, Saint-Claire."

"I'll be waiting," Kyle yelled back.

Eventually, the referee and linesmen ordered everyone but the coaches off the field. It was laughable watching them try to gain control over a game they had lost long ago with their horrendous officiating. Then, just as hostilities seemed to ease, someone from Summit tossed a cup of hot chocolate our way and, again, both sides clashed.

Paramedics were tending to the fat man. He seemed fine—though shaken up and very quiet. At the center circle, Pennyweather and the referee had another heated discussion, but with all the commotion I couldn't hear what they were saying. Then Pennyweather simply shook his head. The referee walked over to our side of the field, stood in front of Kyle, and pulled a red card from his pocket.

"Unsportsmanlike conduct," he said.

Un-fucking-believable.

Kyle threw his arms up, but then, in the next instant, stood tall and didn't say a word. He had composed himself. That was important to Kyle. I know he wanted people to see him as larger than life on the soccer field. He had come up big so often in so many games, it was hard to imagine when he wouldn't snatch victory from defeat. Yet today, we had all witnessed a chink in his armor, a tear in his superhero cape.

The Summit fans started singing, "Na, na, na, na . . . Na, na, na, na . . . Hey, hey, hey, goodbye!" as Kyle walked to our bench and sat down.

He was ejected.

His scoring streak would end.

Worst of all, Millburn would play the rest of the game a man down. I looked at the scoreboard. 7:39 left. If we were able to hold on to the tie, it would still be a disappointment. But if we lost, it would be an utter disaster.

Summit used the man-advantage to flood our defensive zone, penetrating our penalty area with crosses from their wingers and diagonal passes to the middle. Penny-weather directed the team to sit back on defense. Maako and our fullbacks played tough, clearing the ball at every chance, and the two times Summit was able to generate a shot on net, Stuart was there to make the save. We were hanging on. But just barely.

1:11 left.

I was bent over, tugging at the bottom of my shorts. The rest of our players were exhausted, too. As the ball bounced to the corner, Solomon moved too slowly to pick up the opposing winger. The Summit player faked to the inside, stepping over the ball, then cut to the outside. Solomon should have stayed with him, but, instead, he slid desperately, tripping the Summit player to the turf.

"Direct kick," the referee called out, marking the spot of the foul just outside the penalty area.

"Wall! Wall!" Stuart shouted.

Millburn defenders scrambled to set up a line in front of him to block the direct kick.

"Look around!" Pennyweather yelled. "Everyone mark a man!"

On the opposite sideline, the Summit coach was calling for his team to push into the zone. "Set play, set play!"

Stuart checked the angles, and then directed the wall to shift two small steps to the right. The referee blew his whistle. No one had noticed an open Summit midfielder. I pointed and shouted.

"Watch the far post!"

But the Summit midfielder was already sprinting at the goal mouth. The cross was perfect. The ball met his forehead, then the back of the net, a split second before Stuart dove across.

"Shit . . ."

The Summit fans erupted, jumping up and down, screaming and shouting. It seemed everything they did was less for their player who had scored, and more toward Kyle.

Millburn kicked off again, but the last few seconds of the game ticked away quickly and quietly. The Summit sideline buzzed, and streamers of red toilet paper fluttered on the field, long after the final whistle put the 2–1 loss in the record books.

ꟈꟈꟈꟈ

Kyle drove past the ponds along Lake Road. On the Saint-Claires' front lawn, his father was gathering the last of the toilet paper that had been missed earlier.

"Whoa, Jack looks pissed," Kyle said. "He's gonna chew me out."

Despite his words, Kyle didn't seem particularly concerned or contrite. In fact, if I didn't know better, I would've thought he wasn't bothered by the loss at all. I put my hand on the door handle.

"Wait," Kyle said, as he pulled up in his driveway. "Stay in the car a second." He pretended to fiddle with the stereo.

"I heard there were college scouts today," I said. "That why he's pissed?"

"I'll be offered plenty of scholarships. I've got nine or ten coaches calling the house all the time," Kyle said. "No, ol' Jack's gonna chew my ass out because that was *not* how his son's supposed to act." Kyle took on the gruff voice of his father. "Where's the intestinal fortitude? Where's the mental self-control? Are you a Saint-Claire or not, goddamn it?" Then he kind of laughed, but I could tell he didn't really think it was funny. "Let's just wait until he goes inside. Things'll calm down. Jack just needs his Scotch and soda."

Mr. Saint-Claire walked into the garage and stuffed the toilet paper into a garbage can. When he came out, he glanced at the BMW but continued walking toward the front door.

After a minute or so, Kyle and I got out. I grabbed my equipment bag and started down the driveway.

"Kyle," said Mr. Saint-Claire. His voice wasn't particularly loud, but it was completely threatening. "Inside. Now."

I looked back. Kyle's shoulders slumped. He hesitated, then shut his car door and walked up the front pathway where his father was waiting at the door.

STREAKS END!

That was the headline of the *Star-Ledger*'s high school soccer page. The article highlighted Kyle's outburst, pointing out that Summit scored the winning goal after he had been ejected from the game. I didn't mind Kyle taking a hit for losing his cool during the game. It only seemed fair that with the glory came infamy. But what did annoy me was how the article failed to point out that, despite the loss, Millburn still shared the Suburban Conference title, would be seeded second in the next week's Essex County tournament, and, as a result, receive a bye into the semifinals.

What a crappy reporter, I thought.

▢▢▢▢

I spread the newspaper section on the ground, as Annalisa looked over my shoulder. I jabbed an earthworm with a barbed hook, then wrapped it around a few times before piercing the end of its slimy body. Guts spilled out onto the paper.

"Wanna try?" I asked.

Annalisa winced and shook her head.

I walked out onto the dock. I set the bobber a few feet up the line, flipped the trigger on the reel, reached the rod back, then cast it forward. The line whizzed off the spool until the bobber and baited hook splashed in the water. I turned the crank handle and sat down. Annalisa scooted beside me.

"Last night, when we were talking on the phone . . ." I started to say, "it sounded like you were kinda homesick. Are you?"

She leaned into me. "No, I am happy." But the way she said it made me think she was trying to spare my feelings.

I looked at her. "Be honest."

She hesitated, then said, "Things may change soon."

My heart dropped. "Your father's company is gonna bring him back?"

"I do not know for sure."

"But if it does, then your family has to move?"

"*Si.*"

We were quiet for a while. I was upset, but it wasn't Annalisa's fault. I didn't want her to think that I thought it was.

"Well . . . if you might leave someday soon," I said, "then you better tell me all about Arma di Taggia. Where you hung out. What kind of things you did. That way when we send letters, I'll know what you're writing about."

"You want to hear about my home?" she asked.

"Yes."

She smiled, like she thought I didn't mean it.

"Tell me," I insisted.

Annalisa took a deep breath. "It is the most beautiful place in the world . . ." She walked me through the town's narrow streets, and we heard the blaring horns of Alfa Romeos speeding down Via Aurelia Ponente, as young guys tried to catch the attention of the town's women. And we strolled along the seafront promenade from the Annunziata grotto on the one side to the wharf on the other, stopping to listen to the polite discussions of elderly men playing bocce. And she explained how to barter with merchants selling canastrelli biscuits by the park, while we shared orange wedges and breathed in the salty sea air.

Together, through her words, we climbed a hill behind a small hotel, Pensione Sonia, where a garden grew in the middle of a small vineyard. The owner had built a bench made of stones under a wood canopy so his wife could sit and read. That woman passed away a few years ago. Annalisa would go there, especially on rainy days. The old man didn't mind.

I could imagine Annalisa on that bench writing in her journal, surrounded by red poppy flowers and grapevines, sitting alone, and very happy.

"Sounds nice," I said.

"It is special," Annalisa said.

"Special . . ." I nodded. "When I was a kid, I thought this was my special place. And the dock was my throne."

Annalisa laughed. "Your throne?"

"Yeah."

"Like you were the king?"

"Kinda."

"King Jonathan of South Pond," she said.

Long before the ladder, long before the circle, I spent countless summer afternoons at the ponds fishing for bass, sailing model boats, and skipping stones. From the dock, where I could see each cove and curl of the shoreline, South Pond was my dominion.

"I think then I should have a place, too," Annalisa said. "So I may be queen."

"Queen?" I said.

"Annalisa, Queen of . . ." she said. "What about here?"

"Here? South Pond is mine."

"Do not be selfish, King Jonathan," Annalisa said. "You do not need it all, do you?"

"You mean *share* my kingdom?" I said with pretend indignation. "I'll give you North Pond."

But Annalisa shook her head.

"You want South Pond?" I said.

"*Si.*"

"How should we divide it up?"

Annalisa seemed to think about it for a moment and then said, "You could keep all the woods and half the pond from Lake Road to here. I would get all the woods and half the pond from the dock to there." She pointed.

"Where?"

"There," Annalisa said. "What is called the circle, yes?"

I hesitated. "Yeah, that's the circle."

"Is it as special as Stephanie and Trinity say?"

"No, it's nothing special. We could go there now. Just walk right over. It's just a dead end. People make a big deal out of it for no reason." I gestured. "It's right there. Forty or so yards away. Just the end of some no-name street."

"But you have never been there at night?" she said.

I didn't answer.

I was filled with disappointment. I shouldn't have expected Annalisa to be immune to the temptations of sophomore girls. I shouldn't have expected her to be oblivious to what people at Millburn High coveted. Annalisa lived here, interacting, talking, gossiping. It was inevitable that she would shed her innocence. But wasn't anything sacred? Couldn't Trinity and Stephanie have just let her be? They didn't have to fill her head with ideas about the circle. Unfortunately, Annalisa had become more like them than I wanted to believe.

I stared past the far reaches of the pond, beyond the trees, toward the burnt orange horizon. Darkness would be here shortly. I wanted it to come sooner.

"Maybe we can go there one time," Annalisa said. "Could we?"

I reeled in the line. "Yeah, I guess we can go there."

"For a party?"

"Yeah, sure," I said. "For a party."

KYLE AND I ENTERED the locker room. I nodded to Solomon, who nodded back slightly, and then I sat down on the bench in front of my locker. I unbuttoned my shirt and started changing into my practice sweats.

"Real fuckin' funny," I heard Kyle said.

I looked over my shoulder. Taped to his locker was yesterday's *Star-Ledger* article. Kyle tore it off, wadded it up in a ball, then dropped it to the floor. "Who did this?" he asked.

Other players looked up.

"Any of you gonna be man enough to admit it?"

No one said a word until, eventually, Maako spoke.

"The article was right," he said. "You screwed up big-time, Saint-Claire."

"What'd you say?"

"You, Mr. All-State," Maako said, "are the reason we're not undefeated anymore."

"This team wouldn't win half its games without me," Kyle said.

The rest of the players turned.

Maako laughed. "You're such a head case."

Kyle punched a locker with his fist. Everyone stopped what they were doing. The locker room went quiet. "I'm the one who sets everyone else up. I'm the one who scores goals." Then Kyle added snidely, "We can always get another sweeper."

"Blow me, Saint-Claire," Maako said.

Kyle and Maako started toward each other. I stepped in front of Kyle; Brad got in front of Maako. Gallo was in the mix, too. A few others pushed their way into the scrum. I put my forearm hard against Gallo's throat, while he pulled tight on the collar of my sweatshirt. Solomon had ahold of Brad. Kyle and Maako pushed to get close enough to throw a punch, but in the tight space, there was nowhere to go.

Pennyweather burst in.

His face was red and veins rose from his neck. "Are you two gonna toss the season in the crapper because of one loss?" He looked at Maako, then Kyle. "We've got the county semis on Thursday. Win that and we play the finals on Saturday, for God's sake . . . So, do we have a problem?"

"No problem," Kyle said.

"I'm cool," Maako said.

Both of them pulled away from each other and, with Pennyweather watching to make sure things didn't start up again, returned to preparing for practice.

□□□□

On the field, players were passing and trapping. A few were juggling; the rest, stretching. To an outsider, it might've seemed like our team had everything in place for a strong postseason run. We were, after all, Suburban Conference co-champions, seeded second in the Essex County tournament, ranked tenth in New Jersey. But that was just the surface. You had to dig deeper. With two weeks left in the season, a near fight had just flared between our two star players, the hatred between Maako and me still simmered, and, of course, resentment from the backups toward the starters was always present. To top it off, I don't think anyone on the team respected Pennyweather.

Over the past few seasons there had been grumbling about his coaching decisions. From parents. From players. But since the loss to Summit, the criticism had grown much louder. The *Star-Ledger* not so subtly questioned why Pennyweather hadn't taken Kyle out of the game for a few minutes to calm him down. And the *Item* suggested that Pennyweather had been out-coached. I was sure the Millburn soccer powers-that-be weren't pleased. I even heard some of our players guessing how soon after the end of the season he'd be fired.

Fair or not, while Pennyweather had inherited a top program, the margin of error for maintaining the same success was razor thin. It seemed obvious to anyone familiar with our team that an Essex County championship and group state title were all that could save his job.

And judging by the strain on his face, Pennyweather knew it, too.

NICE JOB, JONNY!" a Millburn fan yelled, as I came off the field.

I put my warm-ups on and took a seat on the bench. I had played part of the second and third quarters and most of the fourth; my afternoon was finished. I'd had two shots on net and an assist on Kyle's second goal that gave us a 3–0 margin against Bloomfield. It would've been nice to finish out the game, but Pennyweather apparently wanted the starters back in for the final nine minutes to keep them sharp.

Then the Essex County championship game would be set. Saturday afternoon, four o'clock. Millburn versus

Columbia. For a second year in a row, we'd face our county nemesis.

On the field, Gallo swung the ball to Richie on the right flank. Richie made a textbook chest trap, dropping the ball at his feet. A Bloomfield player came up to face him. Richie drop-passed the ball to Dennis, the trailing midfielder. After beating one opponent, Dennis accelerated down the middle of the field to the top of the penalty area, then delivered a pass to Pete, cutting in from the left side. Pete, however, received the ball less than perfectly. As he tried to regain control, a defender sprinted across the box. Pete's leg swung forward for a shot just as the Bloomfield player's leg swept through for the clear.

Their cleats met.

A split second later, I realized the peculiar sound I'd heard—that everyone on the field and in the stands had heard—was the crack of Pete's ankle. Writhing on the ground, he howled in pain.

Everything moved in slow motion. Guys on the bench immediately stood up to see what had happened. Brad's face instantly went pale. Bloomfield players turned away in horror. Richie stood above Pete, waving frantically to the sidelines. Pennyweather ran onto the field; a medic followed right behind.

When I was alone—in my bedroom, at the pond, in the attic—I'd wonder if everything that had happened before then was just the dormant part of my life, the quiet calm before the spectacular storm. It was my way of dealing with the ladder and the circle and the crowd. Their effects on me couldn't last forever, I'd hoped. At some point, my fortunes had to change. But I don't know if I really knew what I was waiting for. Perhaps some event that would make me feel necessary. To finally be *somebody* in people's eyes. I always figured I'd have to wait until college, or after, for that to happen. When I was with Ruby, I thought it would happen sooner. But she was taken from me, and my hopes were crushed.

Then destiny intervened. Near the end of the seventeenth game of the season, when victory was well in hand, Pennyweather made the decision to put the starting team back on the field. Pete breaks his ankle on a rather ordinary play and, in an instant, forty-eight hours before the Essex County championship game, the dormant time was over.

Someone on the bench nudged me. "Get ready, Jonny."

Everything sped up.

Two emergency personnel gently lifted Pete onto a stretcher. Pennyweather started to walk off the field, his face riddled with alarm. "Stay loose," he said to the starters. When he got to our sideline, he looked down the bench.

"Fehey . . ."

I pulled off my sweat tops and bottoms and ran up to him. He put a firm hand on my shoulder. "Looks like you're our starting striker now," he said. "Get back in there."

ARE YOU READY?" PENNYWEATHER ASKED from behind his office desk.

I nodded.

"No, are you *ready?*"

"Yes," I said.

"I don't mean just physically," Pennyweather said. "You gotta be ready mentally. You gotta take advantage of this opportunity. The team needs you at your best tomorrow—the best you've ever been. I think you need it for yourself."

Pennyweather stood up and walked around to the chair where I was sitting.

"You've come a long way this season, Jonny. You've

got good skills and you understand the game well. But you're not quite there yet. And it's got nothing to do with your legs or your head. It's what's in here—your heart. I don't know if you believe you deserve to start on a championship team. Do you?"

"I think I do," I said.

Pennyweather expected a more forceful answer. "Because if you don't," he said, "then we need someone else to play striker and carry the load."

"I *can* carry it," I said.

"Never be afraid to dream, Jonny." He looked pointedly at the wall of photographs. "Long before any of these guys made it to the level of champion, they had to *dream* of being one. Probably did it day and night. When each was a young kid. Through every club level. Even as professionals on the world's stage. It's no different whether you're playing in the World Cup finals or the Essex County championship. You gotta dream of being a champion with every bit of your heart and soul and guts."

Pennyweather's words usually went in one ear and out the other. But at that moment, I felt a rush of confidence course through my body. Somehow I *knew* my destiny was only one shot away. Pennyweather was dead-on right. I was prepared physically and I was ready mentally. But those were of secondary importance. I had to be able to dream the ultimate dream. I hadn't done that before. But I knew I could do it.

I could make the dream so real that I'd be able to taste it . . .

Smell it . . .

Touch it . . .

Live it . . .

I STOOD IN THE DARK of the attic in a sweatshirt and sweatpants, breathing in the cold air, feeling a slight chill from the floorboards through my socks. I was ready for the starting lineup. I was ready to play Columbia High in the county title game. And now, in a place where I could be anyone, and I could be anywhere, I was ready to dream large.

I dreamed I was Mario Kempes—Argentine soccer god—the man who secured his nation's claim as a South American *fútbol* powerhouse. And this was not an attic in Short Hills, New Jersey, but the campo del Estadio Monumental in Buenos Aires. And it was not the late-season pressure that weighed me down, but the hopes of tens of millions of Argentinos that lifted me up.

25 June 1978. Mundial de Fútbol.

I was el Matador, a flash of céleste and white, slashing through defenders in their solid-orange jerseys. Holanda, led by immortal midfielder Johan Neeskens and forward Rob Rensenbrink, was a proud and worthy opponent. At the end of ninety minutes, the score was tied, 1–1. Extra time had come and, so, el Matador had to seize immortality.

I saw a seam in the defense and called for the *fútbol.* Our fullback delivered the pass hard, the *fútbol* skidding on the grass as I broke toward open space. The Holanda defenders converged. I cushioned the *fútbol* with my instep and pushed it forward down a momentary lane on the right side of the campo. My long dark hair flowing, I ran as I did as a boy on the dirt fields of Córdoba. Neeskens came hard, running step for step, but by the grace of Argentine, I was faster. With a desperate slide, Neeskens tried to cut out my legs. My stride broke momentarily, but I twisted my upper body to maintain balance. I was too nimble to be taken down and the *fútbol* was too much in my control to be knocked away, and it was too much of Argentine destiny for my team to lose. Neeskens was left in my wake.

I raced deep into Holanda territory. Estadio Monumental swelled with anticipation. My winger sprinted down the right sideline, calling out to me.

"Aqui! Aqui!" he shouted.

I pushed a pass his way so he could receive the *fútbol* on the run. Perhaps he thought we could earn a corner kick from this attack. But I wanted more. The Holanda defenders shifted to protect their flank. My winger turned with the *fútbol,* and I gestured.

This was my moment. I ran along the top of the penalty area, received the pass, and then immediately cut toward the goal. A Holanda defender charged me. His cleat caught my back foot, but I kept my balance. Then I avoided a slide tackle from a second defender.

Estadio Monumental sucked in its collective breath . . .

Jongbloed, the masterful Holanda goalkeeper, came off his line, crouching, readying himself. I pushed the *fútbol* with my left foot, but Jongbloed made the save. In the ensuing scramble, I stabbed at the *fútbol* with my right cleat. It bounced toward the goal. For a moment, it seemed the entire world, except the spinning *fútbol,* was still. It was impossible to believe that so much could be gained, and lost, by the final destination of this *fútbol,* but as I watched it find the back netting, I was a believer.

Estadio Monumental erupted!

Céleste and white confetti and streamers rained down from the upper tiers. My run at the goal instantly transformed the campo into a place of baptism, as I passed dejected opponents and was followed by joyous teammates, loping and jumping. I opened my arms and fell to my knees. The heavens had answered.

In the 38th and 105th minutes of the most important match of my nation's history, I scored both the first and clinching goals. In the 116th minute, I sealed the victory with an assist to my teammate and friend, Daniel Bertoni. I was el Matador, and I brought the Mundial de Fútbol home for the first time in my nation's glorious history.

My arms were raised high. They were light, impossibly light, and I huddled, in a swirl of confetti, with my teammates—Passerella, Bertoni, Luque, Fillol, and the rest—and my countrymen and women sobbed, as if their lives were now complete, and children danced and laughed giddily at their feet. I smelled the Rio de la Plata as if it were beneath me . . .

But, eventually, I was pulled away from the campo.

And the céleste and white faded to black.

Cheers softened, then went silent.

Again, I was in the attic.

Standing.

Alone.

But I was no longer an insignificant person, waiting like a mindless drone for my turn in the spotlight. I was Jonathan Fehey, and I was ready to make my soccer dream a reality.

I HAD A FEW MOMENTS before kickoff to take it all in.

Kyle stood beside me, inside the center circle. Richie was on the right wing, Gallo on the left. The stadium lights at Montclair State University rained down on the soccer field; the stands bulged with more than a thousand spectators. One was my mom. I tried not to look in her direction. Or in Annalisa's. Here I was, starting striker for our ninth-ranked Millburn Millers in the Essex County championship game against the fifth-ranked Columbia Cougars. I hoped no one noticed my knees shaking.

Kyle placed the ball on the center mark. "Ready?" he said to me, his breath fogging in the late-afternoon air. "Remember, it's a game like any other, Jonny."

I nodded.

Then he added, "But about a million times more important."

I tried to smile—without much luck.

The referee motioned to the two goalies. "Keepers ready?" Both raised their hands. Then the referee put the whistle to his lips. He checked that both linesmen were in position.

Kyle turned his back to the Columbia players and said, loud enough for only me to hear, "Goalie's out too far." It was vintage Kyle. I knew exactly what to do.

When the referee blew the whistle, I tapped the ball forward and started sprinting. Kyle took possession, dribbled around one Columbia player, then another. We ran stride for stride, just as we did at Christ Church, both of us charging hard, our cleats digging into the turf. An opposing midfielder came up.

"Kyle!" I called out.

The pass came. I pushed the ball back to him with the outside of my foot, threading it between two Columbia defenders. At the top of the penalty area, Kyle reached his leg back and blasted a shot. The ball careened off the shoulder of the sweeper and popped high in the air toward the goal area. I kept running full tilt. I had a chance at the ball. The goalie was coming hard, too. A collision was inevitable, but there wasn't a moment of hesitation in my body or a hint of concern in my mind. I launched myself in the air, my head hitting the ball just as the goalie crashed into me. But this time the wind wasn't knocked out of me and my brain wasn't scrambled. I stayed on my feet and turned to see the ball skip off the top of the crossbar.

There was a loud, "Ohhh . . ." from the Millburn fans.

"Great job, great job!" Pennyweather barked, stalking the sideline.

Kyle ran over. "All game, Jonny. Same thing all game!"

My feet were light, and they stayed that way through the sixty minutes of regulation. Whether it was the field or the crowd or that I had hoped for this opportunity a thousand times, something was different. For one late afternoon, I *was* el Matador.

And just like for el Matador, my moment of glory came a few minutes into overtime. Maako stopped a Columbia attack with a brutal slide tackle, then got to his feet and pushed the ball to Brad, who started up the sideline. Kyle positioned himself at the center circle. Brad cut inside and found Kyle open for the pass.

"Go, Jonny!" Kyle yelled.

Again, I ran parallel to Kyle, knowing he would get the ball to me and I would have to separate myself from the Columbia back line by doing something memorable. A once-in-a-lifetime chance was developing. I'd never get another, I was sure.

Kyle moved the ball down the center of the field, leaving a halfback in his dust. This forced the sweeper to step up. I saw a seam in the defense. At the last possible moment, Kyle slid a diagonal pass. I cushioned the ball with my instep and directed it forward. The goalie charged out, but his effort was in vain. I knew where to put the ball. He couldn't stop me.

And though it all happened in a few seconds, everything slowed down enough for me to catch the Adidas logo spinning forward on the ball and the slight hop the ball took from a divot in the field before I pulled my right foot back and stepped through. The sound of my cleat hitting leather was sublime. It was as magnificent a shot as I had ever taken, starting low and rising.

I watched. From his knees, entangled with the Columbia sweeper, Kyle watched. Players on both teams watched. My mom, the Saint-Claires, hundreds of people from school, our cheerleaders, Annalisa—they all watched, as the ball sailed past the goalkeeper's arms into the upper corner, smacking the netting. Sudden-death overtime was over.

"Yes! Yes!" I bellowed.

I think I was hopping up and down, though I might have been running toward our sideline. I didn't get very far. Richie hugged me first—tackled me, really—and Brad, I think, followed. And then I was buried in a wave of elated teammates.

"We won! We won!" someone was shouting.

Another was screaming like a banshee.

"You're the best, Jonny!" Solomon said. "We're the best!"

And then it all seemed like one loud, happy noise, and everyone on the team, starters and backups—even Maako—was in a tight knot, arms around one another, hollering at the top of our lungs that we were, in fact, Essex County champions.

Kyle grabbed me by the back of my neck. He pulled me in close. "Gonna party with us tonight?"

"Yeah?" I said.

"At the circle, Jonny," he said. "A party at the circle."

❏❏❏❏

After we returned to Millburn High, I sat alone in our locker room. The rest of the team—after laughing and joking, and giving each other high-fives for some time—had gone home. I didn't want to leave just yet. I needed to sit there in my grass-stained uniform, clutching the game ball Pennyweather had awarded me on the bus ride back. On it, he had written today's date and the score.

I tried to remember every bit of what had happened during the game. And in its delirious aftermath, when Pennyweather accepted the championship trophy from the county soccer officials, then handed it to Richie, who passed it to Pete. Pennyweather wanted each of us to have a turn. When the trophy finally came to me, I held it as high as my arms possibly could.

I felt like crying, I really did, just letting the tears flow. The thrill and emotion were so unfamiliar. I'd never experienced anything like this. I got the highest grade on our AP English final last year and I made the honor roll sophomore and junior years, but no one gives a crap about that kind of stuff. And receiving an MVP trophy in Little League—that was so long ago I barely remembered it.

But scoring the winning goal in the Essex County tournament finals—against Columbia, no less—*that* was memorable. Only one person could do that. And it wasn't Maako. Or Richie. Or Gallo. And it wasn't Kyle Saint-Claire. It was Jonathan Fehey.

I had dreamed the dream, then made it come true.

◻◻◻◻

My mom was bubbling over. "Jonny, I'm just so incredibly proud." She must have said it a half-dozen times. "Everyone was cheering for you. My God, it was wonderful. Were all your games as exciting?"

"Today was special," I said, finishing the last of a grilled cheese.

"I had no idea you could run like that," she said. "I

know you practice all the time, but I never imagined you could do all those things with a soccer ball. Darn it, why didn't I bring a camera? I'll have one for next week's game, definitely." Then she looked at me again. But this time it was like she was seeing me for the first time. "You've really become a man. He would've been proud."

I didn't know what to say. I wasn't sure what it meant to be a man. And I didn't really know if my dad would've been proud. I waited to see if my mom would say anything more. A little clarification would've been nice. A lot would've been better. But that was all she had to say.

"I'm going out tonight," I said.

My mom seemed surprised, but pleased. "Going to celebrate?"

"Yeah, I guess." And see Annalisa, I hoped. But I didn't tell her that.

"Where?"

"Just out," I said, stepping into my shoes and grabbing my jacket from the hall closet.

"You'll lock up when you get home?" she said.

I nodded.

I CLOSED THE FRONT DOOR behind me and started across the lawn. Streaks of moonlight broke through a cloudy sky. I saw Kyle's silhouette at the end of his driveway.

"Almost thought you weren't coming," he said.

"Had to throw down some dinner."

Kyle pulled a bottle of Bacardi and a can of Coke from his varsity jacket. "Prime the pump," he said, handing them to me. "Courtesy of Jack Saint-Claire's liquor cabinet."

"Your dad let you take this?"

Kyle looked back toward his house. "What Jack doesn't know won't hurt him."

I poured both in my mouth. The harsh liquor and the

sweet soda ran down my throat. "Where's Stephanie and the others?"

"Don't know, don't really care," Kyle said.

But I knew. Mr. Gianni had been called to a last-minute meeting in Philadelphia for the weekend. I wondered what that meant. Annalisa's mother joined him, leaving her alone in the house. Stephanie and Trinity were probably there with her now.

After another mouthful of soda and liquor, Kyle and I started down Lake Road.

"Why was it such a big deal that I let them come tonight?" he asked.

"You know your sister," I said. "She wouldn't get off my back about it."

"All I know is they better not show up before us. And they better not look like freakers."

I didn't care what they looked like. I just wanted to see Annalisa. I wanted to tell her how incredible it felt to play under the lights, and score the game-winning goal. I figured she'd be excited, too.

Past the entrance to the Short Hills Club, Kyle and I turned into the woods. Faint lights glimmered on the surface of South Pond and I could hear sounds in the distance. My stomach knotted.

"Guess you had it in you, Jonny," Kyle said.

Was there a hint of jealousy in his voice, or frustration

that for the second time in three games he hadn't scored a goal?

"Would've sucked if I missed," I said.

"But you didn't."

At the dock, we continued along the dirt path as it hugged the shoreline. Kyle chugged from the bottle of rum, then handed it to me. There wasn't much left, so I finished it off. Kyle then pulled two beers from his jacket pockets. We stopped and finished those, as well.

Where the path split to the left and curled around the opposite side of the pond, Kyle and I went to the right. We passed through a dense stretch of woods toward a wall of pine trees. Now the voices and music were clear. I drew in a deep breath, letting it funnel through my mouth. At the trees, Kyle pushed through. I followed.

Parked cars lined the cul-de-sac. Under dim streetlights, senior girls passed around liquor bottles and cigarettes, laughing at guys posturing for attention. Everyone from the highest rungs of the ladder was there: Holly McClaren; the Pfister twins, Jules and Jacqueline; Georgie O'Bannon, Millburn's main source for pot; school slut Sheila Mackey; and guys on the football and wrestling teams. At the other side of the circle, standing together, were Tom Blaine, Brandy Stahl, and people from the Glenwood part of town. A black Porsche pulled up. Out stepped Sean McWright, senior class president, and Joshua Schuman, whose family was ridiculously wealthy, even for Short Hills.

I wondered if someone might come up to me and ask what the hell I was doing there. But no one did. Maybe I'd expected too much. Music, alcohol, plenty of pot. It was a party, yes, but not a particularly unique one—except, of course, that I'd never been to one at the circle before.

A few of our teammates were leaning against Maynard's car. Kyle and I walked over.

Richie gave me a high-five. "We're gonna see your goal on *SportsCenter*, Jonny!"

Solomon bear-hugged me. "You did it!"

"I can't believe we beat Columbia," Brad said, handing me a beer.

"Essex County champs!" Solomon shouted. "Let's chug!"

We drank to the offense. And defense. Each of us individually. All the crucial plays. And, of course, the goal I scored. I was amazed at how much the guys remembered from the game, since it was all a big blur to me. I basked in the attention and felt pretty damn certain that it would be a party I'd remember for the rest of my life.

Suddenly, Maako jumped up on the hood of a car, a bottle held high in his hand, and yelled at the top of his lungs.

Holly grabbed the bottom of his pants. "You've had too much, Erik."

"I'll tell ya when I had enough," Maako said.

"Get off my car," she said. "Now!"

Laughing, he climbed down, grabbed Holly tightly, then stumbled forward so that they were almost hidden from the streetlights. He pressed his mouth against hers, but she turned her face, pulled away, and walked off.

"You'll be back," Maako said.

"Over your dead body," Holly said.

Solomon shook his head. "Maako, you're lucky you can play some soccer, because you're a certified, grade-A asshole."

Maako straightened up. "You got it all wrong. On this team I'm the drink that stirs the straw—No, the strink that—Awww, go play wit' yourselves."

"Makes me glad I'm graduating this year," Solomon said. He lifted his bottle. "Another chug . . . To putting up with Maako for only one more week!"

Everyone laughed, and drank.

◻◻◻◻

A few hours later, my head was floating in a drunken haze and my body swayed even when I wasn't moving. I wondered where Annalisa was. She and the other two should've showed up already. I looked around. I must've been doing that a lot, because Kyle knocked me on the shoulder and said, "Everything cool?"

"Yeah, sure," I said.

But I was disappointed. More than a little. Tonight

would've been the perfect opportunity to have Annalisa see me with all the cool people at school, after I had just played the soccer game of my life. It was my time to shine. Later, we could've found a place to be alone.

But just when I figured the three girls had decided to stay home and wait until next year to hang out at a seniors party, Stephanie and Trinity emerged from the woods, glassy-eyed and dressed übergoth (just to annoy Kyle, I was sure), with multiple streaks of color in their black-as-coal hair. Annalisa followed close behind. She looked as pretty as always, though seemed a little cold. I'd offer her my jacket as soon as we had a moment together.

Stephanie and Trinity looked around the party, appearing every bit like lost sophomores. That their typical bravado was nowhere to be found made me chuckle. But my amusement was short-lived. Stephanie saw Kyle, and Trinity saw me, and they instantly took on an air like they very much belonged.

"What's up, Jonny-boy?" Trinity said.

"Not *here*," I said.

This was *my* time. Tomorrow, Trinity and Stephanie could call me by whatever name they wanted, but for one night at the circle I wanted them to fully recognize the respect I deserved.

"Okay, Jonny," she said with surprising contrition.

Annalisa tugged at my jacket sleeve. "*Ciao,* Jonathan," she said, holding tight. I loved the way she said my name.

I loved the way she smelled. I loved looking into her eyes. "You were fantastic at the *fútbol* match. The most—I mean, best—I have ever watched." She draped her arms over me and giggled. "I think I have drinked too much."

I whispered in her ear. "You got your wish."

"What wish?"

"You're at the circle."

Annalisa tilted her head and smiled a very drunk smile. "I believe it is your wish, too."

She was right.

"So, will you mind me, I mean, look after me tonight?" she asked.

I was about to say yes and offer my jacket when Trinity leaned in. "We don't need a damn chaperone. We're big girls."

Stephanie blurted out, "You wanna fool around with Annalisa, don'tcha, Jonny?"

"He does!" Trinity laughed.

Solomon, Richie, and the others turned and gave me a look that all guys understood. "Nice going, Fehey!"

"No, no . . ." I said, without thinking. "I mean—" But my protest had been a little too strong. Stephanie rolled her eyes and pulled Annalisa away.

Of course, I wanted to watch over her. I wanted to kiss her, too. And hold her. I wanted to take her hand and lead her into the woods so we could be blanketed in the comfort of darkness. It wasn't enough to exchange glances and hellos with her in the school hallway. It wasn't enough to spend afternoons sitting shoulder to shoulder in the library stacks, or huddled together on the dock. And, as nice as it was, it wasn't enough to have her voice be the last one I heard before I went to sleep at night.

"Later," Trinity said.

The three girls were off to be in their own world; I was left to mine. I watched as they flitted around the party, talking to senior guys, drinking, smoking, laughing. And flirting—definitely flirting.

The guys on the team went on about the game. There was more chugging and plenty of high-fives. I thought I'd want to hear and talk about my goal and our victory all night long, but I didn't. Instead, I tried to follow whom the three girls were with and what they were doing. But as the night wore on and the alcohol numbed my mind even more, I lost track.

"Who needs another?" Brad said. "I got a full cooler in the back seat of my car—Rolling Rock, Michelob, Heinies." He gestured to his Range Rover parked halfway down the cul-de-sac. "Jonny, you're up." He put a hand on my shoulder and laughed. "You gonna make it?"

I nodded.

"Grab as many as you can," Brad said. "It's unlocked."

I walked—more like staggered—down to the Range Rover. I felt lightheaded (but my legs were heavy) and my vision was frayed around the edges. I was near the point

of no return, but I didn't care. Besides, this wasn't completely unfamiliar. I'd been there twice before. Last spring,
when my mom was on a date, I'd passed out on our roof
with a blanket and a twelve-pack. The other time was with
Ruby. I didn't mind relinquishing control to the alcohol—
what was the worst that could happen?

I put a hand on the car to hold myself steady. I had believed Annalisa and I would end the night together, but
who knew if that would happen now. And if I hadn't been
so drunk, I might've been really pissed off. Instead, I felt
strangely empowered. I decided to have a couple more
beers. Fuck that—I'd have a lot more than a couple. I
was wasted. Now I was gonna get shit-faced. I pulled the
handle on the back door just as someone opened the other
side. We both leaned in.

It was Sloan.

Shit . . .

We looked at each other for an odd moment. "I was,
uh, just gettin' a few beers," I said. "You go first."

Sloan unlatched the cooler top and grabbed a beer in
each hand. The streetlights shined on her blond hair and
glinted in her eyes. She was so good-looking, so popular,
and she didn't give a crap about me. I was just one of
those nameless, faceless, statusless people who took up
space at Millburn High. She started to get out of the car.

But I didn't want to remain nameless and faceless. I'd
been waiting more than a year to say something to Sloan.

"I knew your cousin," I said.

She stopped. "Excuse me?"

"I knew Ruby. We met last summer. Not this past summer, the summer before."

"Why're you telling me?" Sloan said.

"I'm really wasted right now, but I mean it when I tell ya she was the specialist person, I mean, the most special person." *Was* sounded so wrong. "Sorry about what happened." *Sorry* sounded kind of wrong, too.

I expected Sloan to give me a dirty look and walk away. Instead, she sank back into the seat.

I did, too.

And there I was, sitting with Sloan Ruehl in the back of Brad's Range Rover, and the only thing between us was a cooler.

"I miss Ruby," she said. "We didn't get to see each other a whole lot, but when we did, it was wonderful. Like we were sisters. I wish we had been. She was so smart and creative . . ." Her voice trailed off.

There was more I wanted to say, but my thoughts were jumbled. Ruby and I lived a lifetime on that teen tour. I wanted to tell Sloan that, without making it seem like I was trying to win some kind of who-knew-Ruby-better contest. And I didn't want her to think I was just being that loser Fehey, sucking up to her because she was at the top of the ladder.

"In July I visited my aunt and uncle at their lake

house," Sloan said. "Eugene, Ruby's brother—I'm sure she mentioned him—was about to leave for college. Even a year later, they were still all broken up. We went out on their boat a few times. It was nice, but it wasn't the same. All it did was remind me how much Ruby hated—"

"The water," I finished.

Sloan nodded. She handed me a beer. "Please."

I took the opener from the front seat and fumbled to pop off the cap. I fumbled with mine, too.

"To my cousin Ruby," Sloan said, tilting the bottle back. She took a few gulps, then said, "You really knew her, didn't you?"

"I did . . . I think."

"And you liked her?"

"Lots."

"My aunt gave me a bunch of Ruby's stuff," Sloan said. "I kind of wished she hadn't. I didn't want to look at it, but I couldn't get rid of it, either. I mean, how could I? So I got it all in a box under my bed. I wrote 'Ruby' on the side—like I'd ever forget what's in it. A T-shirt from a Divinyls concert's in there and like a hundred photos of us together. And CDs she sent me. We loved the same music. And letters. So many letters. Ruby loved to write."

Someone banged on the trunk. "Hey, Jonny, where's the beer? We're losin' our buzz." Brad looked in. "Whoa, sorry, didn't mean to interrupt."

"Just give us a sec," Sloan said.

I handed Brad as many beers as he could hold, then he walked away.

"Jonny . . ." she started to say. It was the first time I ever heard Sloan say my name.

"Need another opened?"

"I'm okay." She hesitated. "I got one last letter from Ruby. Must've been mailed right before the . . ." Her eyes welled up. "Postmarked from New Mexico. For like six pages she just went on and on. Didn't mention anything else about the trip, just this really great guy from Short Hills. She liked you, Jonny. She said so."

I didn't know if I should've felt happy or sad, but in the condition I was, I doubted I could've felt either.

"Look, I gotta get back," Sloan said. "Do me a favor, don't say anything to anyone. I want Ruby between just you and me."

"Sure," I said.

Sloan got out of the car. Eventually, I did, too. I leaned against the Range Rover, beyond the edge of the party, sucking down one beer . . . then another . . . watching my teammates still celebrating, and Maako with his hands on some girl, and Trinity leaning against Joshua's Porsche, making a fuss about wearing some guy's football varsity jacket, and Sheila passing Brandy a joint . . .

I closed my eyes and drifted, and I would've been happy to just stand there for a while longer, but I had to piss—really, really badly.

I made it over to the pine trees, then stumbled through. I could hardly see where I was stepping. When I reached for a branch I thought was in front of me, I tripped and banged my knee on a rock. I stood up, but then fell again—this time it was my elbow. I staggered deeper into the woods, the surface of South Pond moving closer, the voices from the circle becoming muffled. Finally, I put my beer down, unzipped my jeans, and opened the floodgates.

Maybe it was my mind swirling in alcohol and excitement and the smell of pine, but I was positive something significant had occurred tonight—the ladder had been rendered null and void. The crowd and its power would no longer be an obstacle. I'd entered its temple. Being at tonight's party was surprising, but in a few weeks it'd be expected. Then I'd hang out with Sloan and her bitches any time I damn well pleased.

When I was done, I zipped up and reached for my beer. Instead, I lost my balance, fell forward, and smacked my head against a tree trunk. I tried to straighten up, but when I took a step my ankle rolled sharply on a gnarled root.

Down I went.

The back of my skull hitting the ground.

I reached for my ankle. *Oh, fuck, don't be broken . . . Don't be a torn . . .* Either one and my season was finished. I felt around the bone to gauge the damage, but even the slightest touch hurt like hell. Then I realized my jeans were soaked. *No* . . . I reached under my back and pulled out my beer bottle—empty. I definitely couldn't go back to the party now. Not with a limp and a huge wet stain on my ass. I'd look like an idiot. What, Fehey couldn't figure out how to piss in the woods? People would laugh me out of the circle. Maako would. Sloan would. Trinity and Stephanie would. Who knows, maybe Annalisa, too. I'd be the biggest loser in—

Vomit rushed up my throat. I turned my head and booted. And again. After a few more convulsions, I wiped my mouth on my jacket sleeve and spit.

Why me?

Why tonight?

I laid my head on the dirt. I'd been teased with the belief that my world had changed. A moment of soccer brilliance. In an ideal position for the pass. Receiving the ball perfectly. Striking it perfectly. I scored *the* goal of the season. Because of it, I figured the ladder was crushed and I'd earned the right to hang with the crowd. But it was all a joke. I'd been sucked in, dreaming the dream. Fucked-up ankle. Wet jeans. Stench of beer and piss and puke. Fate got me—hook, line, and sinker.

The clouds parted; the moon shined down. I was alone. In the woods. My head on the cold earth. I was close to the party, not far from my home, and miles beyond wasted. I closed my eyes and let the night pull away . . .

□□□□

"Wasted little girl . . ."

I opened my eyes. Treetops were whipping back and forth and the sky was spinning.

"A little farther," I thought I heard. "Come on, you can make it."

I tried to lift my head off the ground, but couldn't. I turned to my side and looked toward the path. Through fallen branches and between trees, I could just make out the silhouette of a guy walking with a girl. More like carrying her. Toward the rowboat, it seemed. They passed through a thin band of moonlight. I saw the lettering on the back of his jacket. MILLBURN SOCCER. The guy stopped and turned.

Maako.

I held still. Didn't breathe. *Keep going, keep moving . . .* I couldn't let him find me—my world would blow up. He'd accuse me, mock me, say I followed him. Spied on him. Wanted to watch him. I was sick. A queer. A faggot.

He continued down the path, the girl's head bouncing on his shoulder and her legs kind of shuffling along. I closed my eyes. I didn't want to see any more. I didn't want to hear any more. I didn't want to know any more . . .

□□□□

I woke up, again.

Still on the ground.

I looked.

In the dark of the woods, Maako was holding the girl's waist—kind of like they were slow dancing. The pond in the background. Them sucking face (or maybe not). Either way, this was *wrong*. Maako was an asshole—the whole damn school knew it. What girl would've been stupid enough to be alone with him?

The girl suddenly slipped through his arms to the ground. I couldn't see much—her hair billowing, the awkward bend of her knee—but I could tell Maako was standing over her. He had a bottle. He guzzled it. Then guzzled some more. The expression on his face quickly changed. It was peculiar, like he was thinking, figuring, scheming.

He looked toward Lake Road . . .

And up the dirt path . . .

Then the woods . . .

Maako kneeled down. Next to the girl. He was doing something. Lifting her sweater, it looked like. Then maybe her bra. Was he pinching her nipples? Even tugging at them? Yet the girl didn't move, and I didn't hear her say a word.

"Enough, Maako . . ."

But my voice was a whisper, lost in the sounds of the rustling branches. My hands tightened into fists. I felt heat, wicked heat. My fist shot out from my shoulder, crashing against Maako's jaw, feeling the skin and bone underneath give way, blood spurting from his mouth. Maako crumpled to the ground.

It was only in my mind.

I tried to push up off the dirt, but my arms gave way and I collapsed. I was dead tired and so out-of-my-mind drunk. My eyes flickered open and shut. I fought to stay conscious, but a wave of silent blackness rolled over me . . .

◻◻◻◻

"Keep your fuckin' voice down . . ."

Maako's voice shook me awake.

I was face-down on the ground, my mouth pasty, the smell of puke all around. I turned my head and looked. Maako was standing near the dock.

"We were foolin' around . . . She was beggin' for it . . . Take a look . . ."

Who was he talking to? From behind a tree, I saw the silhouette of another guy. I focused my eyes.

It looked like Kyle.

It *was* Kyle.

Shit . . . the Mighty Saint-Claire was going to save the day. Should've expected that. I could hardly lift my head off the dirt, but Kyle was going to swoop in and be a hero.

Maako stumbled over to the girl, then bent down next

to her. "She's passed out," he said. "She won't remember nothin'."

"Why, what'd ya give her?" Kyle said.

Maako laughed. "Harmless stuff." He lifted the girl's sweater. "Take a look."

"Just leave her."

"Ya don't like titties?" Maako said. "That's why ya hang wit' faggy Fehey. You two bone each other, right?"

Kyle stepped toward him.

Maako stood up. "Really wanna fight? 'Cause I'll beat the shit outta ya. Then I'll tell the whole school you're a big homo. Wanna take that chance?"

"You're gonna get kicked off the team."

"By who, Pennyweather? He won't do shit. I'll tell ya a little secret. I don't give a damn if we lose in the state tournament. I got next year to rule Millburn soccer. You seniors'll be gone. Pennyweather'll be gone. That's right, it's a done deal. Pennyweather's finished."

"Bullshit."

"What's bullshit is you wastin' time. Everythin' ya do, the whole damn town knows about. Can't take a dump without the *Item* or the *Ledger* or some other newspaper writin' about it." He motioned toward the girl. "Here's a chance to have a little fun without anyone knowin'. Right here. At your feet. I did her. Now it's your turn."

Kyle said nothing.

Maako laughed. "So you *are* a homo."

"I'll tell the truth."

"What truth?"

"You and her."

"You ain't gonna say a word, Saint-Claire."

"How ya gonna stop me?"

"College scouts'll be at the states," Maako said. "Say a thing and I'll make sure ya don't touch the ball. Me, Gallo, and Maynard'll make ya invisible. We control the game. How's that gonna look to scouts, especially after the shit ya pulled at Summit?" Maako stepped out onto the dock. "I gotta take a leak. Now go be a *man.*"

Kyle stood over her.

No way.

He dropped to his knees.

No way.

He took off his varsity jacket and covered her face with a sleeve.

It was a lie. Kyle wouldn't. Not Kyle.

My eyes had to be tricking me. Or my mind. This was a fucked-up dream. Or nightmare. I couldn't take any more. I turned and let my consciousness spiral away . . .

▫▫▫▫

"I can't do this . . ." Kyle's voice cracked. He sat back on his ankles, between the girl's legs. He wiped his eyes. "I just can't . . ."

I heard the girl cough. Weakly.

Then, her arm flailed. Without warning. Without control.

Kyle's head snapped back. He jumped to his feet, his jeans unbuttoned, and fell back against a tree. I saw a pathetic, panicked look on his face. Then he booted. A bizarre, guttural sound. His body shook a second time. And a third. He touched his forehead, looked at his fingers, then slumped down and buried his head in his hands.

Maako returned from the dock. "Nice goin', Mr. All-State. You're a real fuckin' stud." He stepped past the girl.

Kyle looked at him. "Leavin' her?"

"You got a better idea?"

"We can't."

"I can."

"I can't."

"Then walk her home."

Kyle grabbed his jacket, but stopped. He reached down and seemed to pull the skirt into place, then the sweater down her stomach. He smoothed both of wrinkles.

"Let's go," Maako said.

As Kyle and Maako walked away, I thought I heard something behind me. It might've been a twig snap. Or a falling branch. Maybe a deer finding a place to sleep for the night.

I struggled to turn my head.

A figure moved in the shadows. Maybe.

Or was my mind playing with me again?

When I looked back toward the path, Kyle and Maako were gone.

My head eased back down to the dirt. It was over. The girl and I were the only ones left in the woods. For a final time, I succumbed to the blackness closing in all around my mind . . .

SOMEHOW IT WAS SUNDAY MORNING.

I wished it wasn't.

I was on my bed, looking up at the ceiling, feeling like shit. My head shimmered when my eyes were open, but when they were shut it felt as if my bedroom were spinning out of control.

My tongue felt bone dry and was so swollen it didn't fit my mouth. I tried to swallow. Then tried again. But I couldn't gather any spit, so there was nothing to squeeze down my throat. My arms braced. For a moment, it was like I couldn't breathe in!

Gonna pass out . . .

Gonna—

Air suddenly filled my lungs. I gasped for more. Eventually, my arms eased. And the rest of my body, too.

Then I noticed something smelled putrid. I touched my fingers to my face. What the hell? It was puke. I looked down. I was still wearing my shirt from last night. It was stained. So was my pillow. The horrid taste in my mouth vaguely reminded me of the grilled cheese I ate for dinner, and the beer and liquor that followed. But I wasn't sure exactly what remembering meant, because memories of last night seemed like really bad dreams—fading in, fading out, overlapping, sometimes believable, most times not. I pulled off my shirt, wiped my face, then swept the pillow off my bed.

There was a knock at the door.

"Ma?"

I heard her muffled voice on the other side—at least I thought I did—something about a friend waiting downstairs, waiting for me.

"What, Ma?"

But there was no answer.

Maybe what I thought was my mom's voice was just the rush of heat through the air vents. Or the wind outside. Or maybe it was my mind still sloshing in the backwash at the bottom of that final beer bottle I might've finished, or spilled, or tossed into the woods near South Pond.

I sat up.

Bad idea.

Vomit forced its way up my throat again. I fought it down. I closed my eyes, but that made my head spin more, so I opened them again and waited for the room to settle as much as it would.

▫ ▫ ▫ ▫

Time passed.

I didn't know how much. It was too much effort to even look at the clock on my nightstand. I felt like shit and knew a shower wasn't going to change that a damn bit. I managed to sit up, then put my feet to the floor and stand.

"Ahhh!"

Pain shot up my left leg.

I dropped to my knees and grabbed my ankle. It was swollen, black and blue, and hurt like hell. Was it broken? Was a ligament torn? I tried to remember when and what happened, but couldn't.

Something caught my eye—my uniform and a soccer ball sitting in the corner. I scored yesterday in the county championship game, right? I scored the game-winner, didn't I? The specifics of how I received the ball and the shot I took were muddled. It had been so surprising, so once-in-a-lifetime.

I limped over to the window, pushed open the curtains, and leaned my hands on the sill. It was a raw, blustery morning. No one was on our front lawn, and I didn't see anyone outside the Saint-Claires' house.

Then I heard something behind me.

I turned around, held my breath, and listened.

It sounded like whimpers.

A girl's.

My eyes darted around the room. In the closet. Behind the desk and dresser. Under my bed.

Nothing.

The whimpers grew louder. As they did, it became apparent to me that something more significant than a soccer game had occurred in the past twelve hours. On the floor, my jeans and sweatshirt were strewn about. They seemed damp and were smeared with dirt. A smell of pine and stale beer lingered. So did a sickening sensation. Last night began to piece itself together.

Walking with Kyle . . .

On the dirt path along South Pond . . .

Partying at the circle . . .

Laughing and joking with Solomon and Richie and other guys on the soccer team . . .

Drinking . . .

Hanging out with people in the crowd . . .

Drinking a boatload more . . .

Talking to Sloan Ruehl for a while—Sloan Ruehl for God's sake . . .

Pissing in the woods . . .

Lying face-down on the ground . . .

Did I pass out? Or fall?

And what happened after?

The whimpers, pained and desperate, crawled across the floor, climbed up my body and burrowed inside my mind. I couldn't stop them. Couldn't quiet them. I fell back against the wall and slid to the floor. I put my hands over my ears, but the whimpers scratched my eardrums.

Punishing me.

◻◻◻◻

The bedroom was silent.

My eyes were dry and a searing headache pierced my temples. Twice more I booted whatever was left in my stomach into my wastebasket. I wiped my mouth. I was dizzy and shaking and cold. I shrank within myself, curling up in a ball on the floor, my insides feeling barren. It was late morning, but my room was still dark, and all I wanted to do was sleep for a long, long time.

◻◻◻◻

I sat at the kitchen table, doing my best to swallow half a bagel. My mom seemed upset. She stood at the countertop, spreading tuna fish on pita bread, and said nothing more to me than to ask if I wanted anything else. All I could think about was how the smell of her lunch was turning my stomach.

Eventually, she said, "You left the front door unlocked."

Unlocked? I couldn't remember how I got home. Or how I made it up the stairs to my bedroom. It was just blind luck that I hadn't left the damn door wide open.

"Sorry," I said.

"You drank last night?"

"I was fine."

"That wasn't what I asked," she said. "Did you drink last night?"

"A little."

"Jonny, who do you think you're talking to?" she said. "I wasn't born yesterday. I have a pretty good idea of what goes on at parties . . ."

Not everything. Not last night.

"And I know it includes a lot of beer and liquor," my mom said. "Judging by how you look, I'm guessing you kept up pretty well with the others."

"I'm just tired, that's all."

My head started to throb again. I didn't want to hear any more. I got up from the table. But as I did, the washing machine in the laundry room changed cycles. My mom eyed me, suspiciously.

"Our team photo's tomorrow," I said, though it wasn't true. "We're supposed to wear our home whites. I thought I'd clean mine. I threw in sheets and some clothes, too."

But my mom was unimpressed. She went back to making her sandwich. "I'm doing some grocery shopping later," she said. "If you want me to drop you off at the library, you need to let me know now."

"That's okay," I said.

The library was the last place I wanted to be. A few minutes in the quiet stacks and I'd be ready to pass out. Or, who knows, I might need to boot again.

As I went to leave the kitchen, my mom put up her hand. "I heard you stumble up the stairs when you came in," she said. "I don't want you getting that drunk ever again."

I didn't either.

Then she said, with a seriousness I hadn't heard in a long time, "It's about making the right decisions, Jonny. Every day. In school, at home, or out wherever. I can't always be there. And there's no one else. I have to trust you to do the right thing . . . I don't know if you did last night."

"I did."

That was a lie. I don't think my mom believed me anyway. I would've been better off not saying a word. I walked out, fighting the pain in my ankle, and returned to my bedroom.

◻◻◻◻

I dialed Annalisa's number. I'd lost track of how many times I had. She didn't pick up, yet again, so I left a message.

"Hey, it's me. Hope you had a good time last night. Didn't get to see you much. Sorry for letting Stephanie and Trinity pull you away . . . Pretty crazy night. I got wasted. Not sure I remember most of what happened. Not sure I wanna. Anyway, I guess your parents are back from Philly. You're probably spending the day with them. Any news? If so, I hope it's good news. I guess we'll meet at the library another Sunday. I've got some stuff to sort out anyway. Call me when you get home."

I hung up.

When the dryer finished, I put the sheets back on my bed and folded my clothes, then spent much of the afternoon sitting in front of my bedroom window with a bag of ice on my ankle. The swelling had started to come down. I'd look over at the Saint-Claires' house. Kyle hadn't gone outside at all. Not for a run. Not for a drive. Not for anything.

Later, after my mom left, I hosed out my wastebasket and taped my ankle tightly, then took a walk to South Pond. I followed along the path, careful not to take an awkward step. As I approached the dock, I could see the circle through the pine trees. Without parked cars or people partying, it seemed so benign. I stopped near the rowboat and looked around. I wasn't sure what I expected to find. Empty beer bottles . . . remnants of vomit . . . pee-stained trees? But it all appeared untouched. Just a stretch of woods like any other stretch of woods.

I kneeled down, scooped dirt in my hand, and lifted it to my nose. The smell was familiar. It stirred uneasiness in my gut, while my mind started to churn.

What made a friendship? Being alike? Thinking alike? Hanging out together? Doing things? Talking about deep stuff? Did my friendship with Kyle answer "yes" to any of these questions?

Did it matter?

Maybe friendship was something more amorphous, with vague boundaries that changed over time, depending on comfort, jealousy, anger, affection, and every shade of emotion in between.

I'd always believed no person could "know" me. No matter how much we talked, no matter how much time we spent together, no matter how close it seemed we were. I had secrets. I had feelings and thoughts and dreams and fears that I'd never share, that no one would be able to uncover. Some were simple and innocuous; others were complicated and serious. A few were disturbing. And if I lived to be old, none of them might ever surface. Even with the minute chance that one did, it might never be witnessed by another person. So, in the end, people knew only what I wanted them to know. I coveted that secrecy. It was what made me, me.

In the hours that passed, as I watched the sunlight fade and dusk turn to night, I came to the conclusion that all that had been true for me was undoubtedly true for Kyle, too.

A thousand times I questioned if it could possibly have been someone else in the woods with Maako last night. I conceded that I had been insanely drunk. And I conceded that I couldn't have trusted my bleary eyes to see with certainty through the trees and darkness. And I conceded that in the deepest, most envious part of my mind, I had hoped to God that I would someday witness Kyle do something so wrong that he'd fall monumentally from the pedestal he had such a firm footing on.

Still, each of those thousand times, the answer was the same.

It had been Kyle.

I saw him.

He hurt that girl. And Maako did, too.

I OPENED THE PASSENGER DOOR and stepped in. Kyle nodded. I did the same. Neither of us said a word. I noticed the car stereo wasn't on and Stephanie wasn't in the back seat, but I didn't ask about either.

We took off down Lake Road, the morning sun reflecting a harsh glare on the BMW's windshield. We passed the Short Hills Club entrance, then the ponds. A little farther, the car rumbled over Redemption Bridge.

"Gonna talk?" Kyle said.

"What do you want me to say?"

"I don't know. Something."

"It's Monday morning, and I'm beat."

"And you're in a shitty mood," Kyle said. He gestured toward my leg. "Hurt yourself?"

"No, why?"

"Thought I saw you limp."

"My leg's fine," I said. "In fact, both are fine." I pointed to his forehead. "What's up with that?"

He touched the gash with his fingertips. "Didn't notice it."

"Doesn't look too good."

"It's nothing."

"How'd it happen?"

"What's the difference?" he said. "Probably happened during Saturday's game. Those assholes from Columbia were taking a lot of cheap shots. It was brutal out there."

"Yeah, I know," I said.

Kyle had a look on his face as if he suddenly realized I'd played as much of the game as he had.

"Maybe I got it on the way to the party," he said.

"I don't remember that."

Kyle was getting pissed off. "Okay, so it was on the way home. A low branch. Walked right into it."

"A branch?" I said.

"A branch," he answered.

Kyle wanted me to say something more. He wanted me to push him. And I wanted to challenge him. I wanted to get past any bullshit story he might offer. People at school thought Kyle could do no wrong. They were fortunate; they saw only that side of him. I needed to find out if Kyle would admit to me—his supposed best friend—the truth about what happened. If he didn't, then Kyle was a bold-faced liar and our friendship wasn't worth crap. If he did, then we faced even bigger issues.

"Maybe something else cut you," I said.

Kyle smacked the steering wheel with his fist. "What's up your ass, Jonny?"

"What?"

"You're acting as screwed up as my sister. Who knows what's wrong with her? Too sick to go to school—I doubt that very much. My parents wanted to know if I gave her anything to drink. You were there. After she showed up, I didn't see her the rest of the night." Kyle gave me a snide laugh. "If that isn't enough, now I gotta deal with you and your problems."

"I don't have any problems."

"Then why'd you leave the party early?"

"It was late," I said.

"Late?"

"Yeah."

"You left without saying a word."

"I was tired."

Kyle's jaw clenched. "Maybe you left early 'cause you got shit-faced. Your problem, not mine. Maybe you left early 'cause you didn't get enough attention. Again, your problem, not mine. Maybe you're pissed at me for bringing you—"

"You didn't *bring* me," I snapped.

"Yeah, Jonny, I *did*."

There he was, baiting me. Kyle knew damn well everyone in our grade had his or her place. He was quick to remind me of mine.

"You wanna be the big man now?" Kyle said. "Fine, you're it for a couple of days. But that goal better not've gone to your head. It's real nice that you started one game and scored one goal, but don't get all crazy about it. I'm *not* gonna kiss your ass, if that's what you want."

"Yeah, that's what I want." I didn't hide my sarcasm.

We were quiet for the rest of the ride. I stared out the passenger window as we raced down Highland Avenue, passed under the trestle at the Short Hills train station, and made a left at St. Rose onto Millburn Avenue.

Kyle turned down the high school driveway and skidded the BMW into a parking space. We both got out.

"Jonny, do me a favor," Kyle said.

"What?"

"Find another ride from now on." He slammed his door and walked off.

◻◻◻◻

I started toward the high school main entrance. At the front doors, I looked up at the stone facing.

ACADEMICS • ATHLETICS • INTEGRITY

I had never really noticed the words before. People passed by, but I didn't see them. They were talking, but I didn't hear them. Then someone patted me on the back.

"Great game, Jonny!"

I felt a hand on my shoulder.

"Incredible goal!"

Someone tugged on my sleeve.

"Fehey, you're a soccer stud!"

"We're gonna start calling you 'Super Foot,'" another said.

People were looking at me. Seniors. Juniors. Sophomores. People I knew. Many I didn't. Saying they had been at the game. That they had read the article and saw the photo of me in yesterday's *Star-Ledger*. Offering congratulations. Another pat on the back. A friendly knock on the shoulder. Someone wanting a high-five. They didn't whisper behind me; no one looked indifferently toward me. They were crowding me . . . pushing me along . . . funneling me through the doors.

Inside the school, the PA system crackled.

"Attention, students . . . The date for the SATs is Saturday, November fifteenth . . . The doors will

*open at seven thirty a.m. . . . Congratulations to
the varsity soccer team winning the Essex County
title . . . A big cheer for Jonny Fehey who scored
the winning goal . . . On Wednesday, there will be
a ceremony to place the team trophy in the Hall of
Champions display case . . . "*

The hallway continued to buzz with conversations. People
were walking this way and that way. Locker doors were
opening and closing. This was insane. Didn't anyone realize what happened this weekend? And I'm not talking
about some damn soccer game.

Of course, no one could've known. If the girl walked
past me right now, would I even recognize her? Could I
see beyond whatever expression was on her face and
know the hurting underneath? I looked around me. I saw
one girl. Then another. Then every girl within my view.
All with smiling, laughing, happy faces.

▫▫▫▫

I was running hard, but not really. Trying to make the effort look good, knowing it was bullshit. The ball came to
me on a pass from Richie. It bounced off my cleats as if
they were made of stone. I recovered, sort of, and dropped
a pass back to Kyle. It was all I felt capable of doing—
giving up the ball as quickly as possible. Only two days

ago, I'd scored the sudden-death overtime goal to win the county title. I should've been flying high, enjoying the defining moment of my life.

Pennyweather slammed his clipboard to the ground. "What the hell's going on?"

Players stopped and stood, fists on their hips.

"Some of you guys are going through the motions. Fellas, if you think the state title is just gonna be handed to you, you're woefully mistaken." He stared at each of us. "Didn't we learn a lesson at Summit? *Every* team that makes it this far is talented. It's the one with the hungriest players that wins . . . Kyle, you with us today?"

He had his head down. "Yeah."

"Sure as hell doesn't seem it," Pennyweather said. "Tell me, is there anything more important in your life than the next two games?"

"No," Kyle said.

"You and a few others are practicing like you're worried more about chasing skirts and drinking booze. I'm sure you did enough of that over the weekend. Fellas, the semifinals are on Friday. Think about that—the state semifinals. Win that, and you play in the finals the next day. Win that, and each of you will get to hold the goddamn state championship trophy."

But the team was unmoved, and Pennyweather knew it.

"Know what? I've lost my patience," he said. "You're

gonna run laps for the rest of the afternoon. Maybe tomorrow'll be better. Start fresh. Practice like gang-busters and we'll be fine. But if you don't, I'll have the team run the snake so long and hard you'll be too tired to even think about girls, or any other goddamn thing. Now get your asses moving."

Players grumbled, a few cursed, but the team quickly formed a line and started jogging down the field. Kyle was a few steps ahead of me.

Maako came up next to him. "Get your shit together, Saint-Claire," he hissed.

▫▫▫▫

"Hey, Annalisa," I said. "Didn't see you in school again today. You're not avoiding me, are you? Just joking. If it's nice tomorrow, maybe we can meet on the patio. I wanna talk . . . Gonna go to the game on Friday? Hope so . . . Call me later."

I hung up the phone.

Leaving yet another voice message.

I wished she had answered. I wanted to hear her voice. I liked how she said certain words, and how she some-times mixed in Italian with her English. We could've talked about silly stuff. Like boring classes and annoying teachers. What a relief that would've been. I had had enough with serious shit. My mind was fried. I just couldn't stop thinking and thinking and thinking.

I turned out my bedroom light. Something had to be done. But I didn't know what it should be. Hopefully, an answer would come to me. Hopefully soon.

I KNOCKED ON PENNYWEATHER'S office door.

No answer.

I knocked again and waited, just to make sure.

A few minutes earlier, I watched Pennyweather go into the teachers' lounge for his Tuesday departmental meeting. But he could be back at any time. I turned the knob, stepped in, and closed the door behind me. My heart was beating quickly, but not urgently.

I searched the bookshelves crowded with computer language manuals and teaching textbooks, but didn't find it there. I scanned the wall, yet there were only the framed photographs and autographed soccer ball I had marveled at the last time I was in the office. They were of no interest now. I walked behind Pennyweather's desk. On top sat a stack of papers marked, "To Be Graded." I opened the left desk drawer. Just file folders. I opened the right drawer. There it was.

The championship trophy.

It was made of polished brown wood, with a base so it could sit upright. At the center was a gold plate engraved with the words PRESENTED BY THE NEW JERSEY STATE INTER-SCHOLASTIC ATHLETIC ASSOCIATION TO THE ESSEX COUNTY BOYS' SOCCER TOURNAMENT CHAMPIONS. Its final destination was to be the display case outside the gymnasium entrance, where all Millburn sports championships were honored.

I stuffed the trophy in my backpack, closed the drawer, then checked to make sure I hadn't left anything out of place. I opened the office door a crack and listened. I didn't hear anyone coming, so I swung my backpack over my shoulder and stepped out as nonchalantly as possible. A couple of sophomore guys were horsing around at the end of the hall, but they didn't notice me.

ロロロロ

I stood at the shoreline of South Pond. The circle's street-lights glimmered on the mirrored surface. I opened my backpack and pulled out the trophy, a roll of athletic tape, and the game ball that Pennyweather had awarded me.

I pierced the ball with a penknife, then squeezed it

flat. I found a good-sized rock, wedged it against the ball, then placed both on the gold plate. I pulled the tape tightly around once. Twice. Then a third and fourth time. When the rock still wasn't secure enough, I continued until the tape ran out and all that was left was the cardboard dispenser.

I waited for a moment of reconsideration.

None came.

It was too late for that. After what happened at the circle on Saturday night, Kyle and Maako didn't deserve to have the trophy on display. That was my decision. Someday the rest of our team might find out why. Maybe they'd understand; maybe they wouldn't. I didn't care either way.

I held the trophy, rock, and game ball in my hand, swung it back and forth—the way we had learned to throw the discus in gym class—then heaved it toward the middle of the pond. It didn't go very far, but it went far enough, disappearing into the inky black water, sending ripples out in ever-widening circles until they reached the toes of my cleats.

BY NEXT MORNING, NEWS that the trophy was missing had spread quickly. I stood outside the cafeteria entrance with Solomon and Brad and watched their reaction to the PA announcement that the Hall of Champions ceremony had been canceled.

Solomon threw his hands up. "Are you kidding me?"

"No trophy, no ceremony," Brad said.

"This sucks."

"Maybe the athletic department will get us a replacement."

Solomon shook his head. "I'd bet anything *he* lost it."

"Who?" I said.

"Pennyweather."

"Yeah, he decided to keep it," Brad said with a laugh. "He knows it'll be the last county title he wins at this school."

There was a commotion at the other end of the hallway. It sounded like someone punched a locker. People stopped and stared. A few craned their necks. I looked, too. I wasn't surprised to see that it was Kyle. His eyes were wide and his hands tightened into fists.

"What's with him?" Solomon said.

"Who knows?" Brad shrugged.

"Something's been up his ass all week."

Brad gestured to me. "You wanna go see?"

"No," I said.

"I guess I'll go, then," he said.

Brad walked down the hall. When he got to Kyle, he put his hands up in a calming gesture. They started talking. While they did, I watched for Annalisa. I still hadn't seen her all week, and with Stephanie and Trinity both out supposedly sick, I wondered if the three of them were together somewhere. The thought of that bothered the hell out of me. Who knows what garbage they might be filling her head with.

Soon, Brad came back. He had a smirk on his face.

"So what's the story?" Solomon said.

"His BMW's gone."

□ □ □ □

"Thanks for the ride," I said. "Again."

My mom gave me one of those motherly smiles. I think she knew something was going on between Kyle and me, but she hadn't said anything. Over the years, he and I had been in plenty of arguments. I think she figured this was just another that would eventually blow over. Or maybe she was too tired after a long day of work to be overly concerned.

I stared out the passenger window as we drove up Highland Avenue and, eventually, turned onto Lake Road. Soon we crossed over Redemption Bridge and passed the two ponds. When we came to our house, I saw Kyle's BMW in the Saint-Claires' driveway. It seemed fine.

What a joke, I thought. Kyle made such a big deal over nothing.

My mom and I went inside. I took a long, hot shower, trying to wash away another lousy practice, another lousy day. It wasn't helping much. Afterward, I dried myself off and put on sweats. I sat down at my desk. Still no messages on my answering machine. I had finished the application for Wesleyan, but there were others. Plenty of others. I pushed the pile aside. I was hungry. Or maybe I just needed a distraction.

I walked out of my bedroom and heard my mom and Mrs. Saint-Claire talking in the living room. When I got halfway down the stairs, they stopped.

"Hello, Jonny," Mrs. Saint-Claire said. Her eyes were red. "Excited for Friday's game?"

"I guess."

"Want some dinner?" my mother asked.

I nodded.

"Give us a few minutes," she said.

I returned to my bedroom and closed the door—loud enough for them to notice—but in the same motion, I pushed the door open a little. I put my ear toward the hallway.

"What a mess today," I heard Mrs. Saint-Claire say. "Steph asked me to drive her to school, which was fine. We talked a little in the car and she gave me a kiss when I dropped her off, so I thought, after being too sick to go to school on Monday and Tuesday, everything was back to normal. Around ten, I get a call from the main office asking when Steph would be returning. I told them she was already there. They assured me she wasn't. I immediately called Jack. We found out Steph took the keys to Kyle's car. She and that Trinity drove out to Passaic."

"Passaic?" my mom said.

"I know, I know. And neither of them has a license."

"Why did they go all the way to Passaic?"

"St. Mary's Hospital."

"A hospital?"

"Their friend . . ." Mrs. Saint-Claire seemed to choke up. I opened the door wider. "If you'd ever seen this girl . . . She was just so delicate. It's so terrible to say . . . She tried to hurt herself."

"Hurt herself? Who?"

"Their new friend," Mrs. Saint-Claire said. "Annalisa."

I started to tremble.

Then my stomach quaked. I felt like booting.

Visions from last Saturday night came at me with a vengeance. The sounds were sickeningly familiar. A girl's whimpers. They bled. They were chaotic. They echoed, rattling my skull. I shut my eyes, but they grew closer.

Like the girl was near me . . .

Like she was beside me . . .

Like she was inside my head . . .

"Stop . . ." I heard myself say. "Make them stop . . ."

But they didn't.

I opened my eyes.

Annalisa was in front of me. Spread out on the ground, her plaid skirt pulled up high, her hair caught on a fallen branch.

Why didn't I do something . . . say something . . . make a noise . . . throw a rock . . . anything?

How pathetic.

"When they saw bandages on her wrists," Mrs. Saint-Claire was saying, "that's when Trinity lost it. Steph was able to hold it together—but that doesn't surprise me. She's got this inner strength that Kyle doesn't even have. Steph said she sat on the bed, hugging Annalisa, with tears running down her cheeks. She just kept telling Annalisa, 'We love you . . . We love you . . .' Then the nurse came in and told them time was up. Somehow they made it back to Short Hills. Apparently, Trinity cried the whole way. Steph left Kyle's car in the driveway, and the two of them went to the creek. That's their place, I guess . . ."

▫ ▫ ▫ ▫

The front door closed.

I was sitting against my bedroom wall, my eyes shut, my head throbbing. I got up, put on my sneakers, and stepped down the stairs.

"Jonny . . ." My mom's voice startled me. I looked in the living room. She was sitting in the same chair. "Do you know a girl named Annalisa?"

"Yes," I said.

"You know her well?"

"Sort of."

My mom kept staring at me.

"She's nice," I said. I don't know why I chose the word "nice," but to say nothing seemed to betray the time we'd spent together. And, yet, saying "nice" did exactly that.

"Do you know what happened to her?"

"What do you mean?"

"Something bad happened to her."

"Oh . . ." I said. "Sorry."

"So, you do know?"

"No, Ma, I don't."

Could she see something in the paleness of my face? Could she read my bloodshot eyes? Was my slumped posture a dead giveaway? She turned from my direction.

"I just wanted to make sure," my mom said.

I crossed the hallway. "I'll be back later," I said.

As I closed the front door behind me, I heard her say, "It's a terrible shame . . ."

▫▫▫▫

The Giannis' house was dark.

I stood across Highland Avenue, leaning against a tree at the edge of a neighbor's lawn, stepping back into the shadows to conceal myself whenever a car's headlights came in my direction.

Things could be the way they were before, and I wouldn't let anything happen to Annalisa ever again. I'd promise that with all my heart. We'd go back to exchanging smiles on the patio and talking on the phone until all hours at night. We'd meet at the library. And the dock. And sneak into the back stairwell at school. Annalisa affected me. She touched me. She held my curiosity. Whether it was her accent, or the way she moved, or the comfort she gave me whenever we were together. I wasn't done enjoying all that. I didn't want things to change. I wouldn't let them.

But those thoughts made me feel foolish. Nothing

would be the same again. Not Annalisa. Not Kyle. Not me. Saturday night could not be done over or erased or ignored.

I waited hours for a light to go on in the house, but none did. It was cold and I was well past exhausted. So I walked back home and spent hours staring at my bedroom ceiling. At some point I fell asleep, but by then a seething anger had infected me. It filled my mind until I couldn't think of anything else.

Something had to be done.

And I knew I had to do it.

AP EUROPEAN HISTORY ENDED, but I was in no hurry to leave. It had been that way all day—waiting for one class to end and the next to begin. I sat at my desk, my mind wired, my body on edge. I stared out the window. In the distance, something caught my attention—Kyle crossing the football field toward our locker room, with Maako right behind him.

I bolted from the desk, grabbed my books, and sidestepped past the last few people at the door. I raced down the hallway to the stairwell, grabbed the handrail, and skipped down the stairs, hitting the first-floor landing hard. I pushed through the side exit that led to the athletic fields behind the school and sprinted along the fenced perimeter of the running track. As I came around the back of the football stadium stands, Kyle and Maako were facing each other.

"You've been talking," Maako said.

"Give it a rest," Kyle said.

Maako crashed his fist into Kyle's cheek, sending him to the pavement. I expected Kyle to jump to his feet and give Maako the fight of his life. Instead, he stayed down, wiping gravel off his face.

I tossed my books and ran as fast as I could.

Maako grabbed Kyle by his sweatshirt, lifted him to his feet, and then threw him against the stadium wall. "Shut. Your. Mouth." For a second time, his fist slammed into Kyle's jaw, dropping him to his knees. "No one knows," Maako said, standing above him. "Let's keep it that way." Then he took Kyle's head and smashed it against his knee. Kyle fell backwards.

"Hey, asshole!" I yelled.

Maako laughed. "Look, it's your girlfriend, Saint-Claire."

Kyle put his hand up. "Jonny, you don't need to be here," he said, spitting blood on the wall as he walked away. I went to follow him, but stopped. Kyle and I would face each other another time.

My business here wasn't finished. I turned and smiled my most enraged smile.

"Run along, Fehey," Maako said.

I shook my head and I started toward him.

"What're you gonna do?" he questioned.

My hands curled into fists. "Give you a beating."

"Faggy Fehey, you lost your mind. Did you somehow morph into a tough guy when I wasn't looking? Take a chill pill before I teach you a lesson. Got it?"

I hit Maako with my shoulder and lifted him high in the air. He swung wildly with his right hand into my ribs. Then his left. Then his right again. I dropped him to the ground, but he managed to regain his balance. He lunged at me, throwing a punch at the same time that connected with my chin.

Flash—

This was familiar.

My consciousness started to dim, but not completely. I staggered back against the wall. For some reason, Maako didn't come after me. I blinked a few times to clear my head. I was going to make him regret that decision.

"Done?" Maako asked.

I threw an overhead right, grazing his jaw, then dove at his legs, knocking Maako to his back. Before he could turn, I sat on top of his chest and rained down punches— left, right, left, right, left, right. He covered up. Most hit his forearms, but a few smacked his face. The impact of my fist and the bounce of his head against the pavement were things of beauty.

"Ahhhh!" Maako yelled, throwing me off with his hips. I got to my feet. He got to his. His face was a mess. A cut

above his eyebrow was pouring blood, both cheeks were raw, and there were two huge bruises on his forehead. My savagery surprised—and pleased—me.

The momentary letdown was a mistake. Maako bull-rushed me, knocking me against the wall. Using his arm like a club, he chopped down on my head, again and again. I threw an uppercut to his jaw, but Maako returned with a punch dead on. My nose exploded with blood and my eyes swelled with tears.

Maako reeled backwards and dropped to a knee. Then he simply sat down. He was finished. I was finished. We didn't need to throw any more punches—at least not today. We didn't need to hurt each other any more. I looked down at my shirt. It was torn and dirty. I could feel a dribble of blood on my chin.

It felt good.

Maako had a glazed look in his eyes. He was touching the welts on his forehead and wiping away gravel. He spat a wad of bloody phlegm on the ground. The knuckles on his hand were torn up.

Kids ran toward us. A couple of teachers, too. They were yelling something about us being insane. Before anyone got close enough to hear, I said to Maako, "Bet you had a good time Saturday night . . ." I coughed. "Near the dock . . ."

Maako pulled a tooth from his mouth and tossed it away. "You saw?"

"I did."

"Everything?" Maako said.

"Yeah."

"Then you know," he said, spitting again. "Say a word and Kyle's done. Fight me all you want, but it won't protect him."

I stood up straight. "You're such a loser."

Maako half laughed. "A loser?"

"I didn't do this for Kyle."

ロロロロ

Pennyweather was shouting, really going berserk. Veins rose from his neck and spit flew from his mouth. I didn't think it was particularly funny, but I wasn't especially concerned, either, mostly because my thoughts weren't entirely coherent. Besides, I relished having beaten the snot out of Maako, and, in a perverse way, even having had the snot beaten out of me.

"What were you two thinking? No, don't bother answering that," Pennyweather said. "I told you a month ago to let go of this personal crap. You don't have to love each other. You don't have to like each other. You don't even have to acknowledge each other. But, for God's sake, you can't fight each other."

He grabbed some magazines and threw them at us. Pages tore and the covers came off a few. The outburst didn't faze me.

"Does this have anything to do with the missing trophy?" Pennyweather said. "Does it?"

I shrugged.

Maako just sat there.

"Fine, play dumb," Pennyweather said. "I want to keep you both out of the entire game tomorrow—yes, the whole goddamn game. But we can't afford that. And I'm not gonna punish the rest of the team for your stupidity. I'm gonna do the next best thing—both of you will sit the first half. If we get behind—I don't care what the score is—then so be it."

Pennyweather stood behind his desk, arms folded, his tie undone. His voice was a normal volume, but no less menacing. "If we lose . . ." He kind of laughed and shook his head. "If we lose, it's gonna be on your heads. I'm not taking the fall for this. There are consequences." He turned away from us and stared out the office window. "Now, get the hell outta here."

I left first.

Moments later, I heard Maako's steps behind me.

▫▫▫▫

"I'm sorry, sir," the woman said.

"You can't put me through to her room?" I asked a second time.

"No, I can't."

"Why not?"

"Sir, please calm down."

"Can you at least tell me if she's a patient? Last name is spelled G-I-A-N-N-I."

"It's hospital policy not to give out that information," the woman said.

"Hospital policy? This person is really important to me. I need to know if she's a patient in your hospital, but you're telling me you can't because of some ridiculous policy?"

"Yes," the woman said. "That's what I'm telling you."

"So that's it?"

"I'm afraid so."

I hung up the phone and threw it into the pillows on my bed.

Pennyweather kept his word.

Maako and I sat at opposite ends of the bench for the first half of the state semifinals against Randolph. After scoring the game-winner last Saturday, I should've been hungry to get on the field and break the 1–all tie. I should've been chomping at the bit to prove my play against Columbia hadn't been a fluke. But I wasn't.

And while I did start the second half, I might as well have been at home on our couch. My head wasn't in the game, and I had no feel for the ball. Halfway through the third quarter, Solomon made a perfect chip pass over the Randolph back line that sprung me for the goal, but my shot sliced way off to the right. A few minutes later, I dribbled a breakaway out-of-bounds. The rest of the time, I was lost. Even with the cheers and clapping from the Millburn fans, my mind and body had betrayed me.

Pennyweather eventually pulled me from the game. "Wasn't your afternoon, Jonny," he said as I passed him on the way to the bench.

The team scored three goals in the fourth quarter, advancing to the finals with a 4–1 victory. Stuart was brilliant in net and Solomon had the defensive game of his life. Dennis put one in. Richie did, also. Kyle had the other two, including the game-winner. He was back on track.

Some things never change.

□□□□

When the team bus returned to the high school, Pennyweather took me aside. "Great game the team played today," he said, putting a hand on my shoulder.

I nodded.

"Look, Jonny, I'm not gonna sugarcoat this," Pennyweather said. "We're gonna try a different lineup for the finals . . ."

He went on about starting just two forwards because he thought our offensive zone was getting clogged with players. It was coaching bullshit. I knew what he was getting at. I had played myself out of today's game and he couldn't take a chance that I'd do the same tomorrow. He told me to be prepared to come in off the bench, but I knew he said it more out of obligation than really meaning it.

"Sure," I said. "I'll be ready."

Pennyweather looked at me. He seemed genuinely disappointed. Maybe he expected me to bitch and moan, or give him some song and dance to convince him otherwise.

"I know you've had something on your mind all week," he said. "If you wanna talk, my office door is always open."

I didn't say anything.

"Guess it wouldn't help if I told you to put it aside until after the championship game," Pennyweather said.

I shook my head. "I don't think so, Coach."

SATURDAY MORNING'S GAME WAS GOING to be a coronation. That's what the *Star-Ledger* wrote. It was what the town expected. The game in which Kyle Saint-Claire would lead Millburn to the Group III state title and a top-five final ranking in New Jersey.

He didn't disappoint.

On a frigid, damp field at Seton Hall University, Kyle scored on a second-quarter penalty kick to break a scoreless tie with Rahway, then a few minutes later delivered a crisp give-and-go pass that Brad buried into the net. In the final quarter, with storm clouds on the horizon, Kyle drilled a shot from twenty yards out that left the Rahway goalkeeper pounding the turf in frustration.

When the referee blew the final whistle, Millburn players and their families, classmates, and fans all stormed the field. At the center of the celebration, Kyle was hoisted onto Richie's and Solomon's shoulders. He raised his arms high.

I stood off to the side. People patted me on the back, offering congratulations. That I was now part of a state championship team didn't matter much. But I feigned a smile anyway.

I didn't take the team bus back to the high school. Instead, I walked off the field toward the university parking lot where my mom was waiting. I couldn't tell if she was happy that we had won, disappointed that I hadn't played much, or confused that I wasn't excited like everyone else.

"Do you want to stick around awhile?" she asked.

Looking back at the mob of people on the field, I saw Kyle take turns embracing Stuart, Brad, Gallo, and even Maako. For an instant, Kyle looked at me. His smile withered the smallest bit. Or maybe it was just my imagination.

"No," I said. "Let's go."

□□□□

I stood outside our house.

I had no place to go and nothing in particular to do; I

just didn't feel like sitting in my bedroom. So I wandered around the backyard, tossing pine cones, picking at tree bark ... and thinking. Lots of thinking. About Annalisa.

By the end of the week, people at school noticed she hadn't been to class. Rumors ran rampant. One had her tripping on the way home from the circle and messing up her face—now she was in post-op at Overlook Hospital. Another had her parents sending her to a rehab center in Manhattan. The most popular one claimed Mr. Gianni had been called back to Sicily because the feds were closing in. People were so glib. If they only knew the truth.

I had circled the house a few times. Eventually, I took a seat on the curb. Soccer season was finished. I wasn't sure that had sunk in yet. It had been the bond between Kyle and me. Training each August; playing on the school team each fall. It was what kept our friendship intact. Where did we go from here? I wondered.

I rummaged the pavement for a handful of pebbles. A few cars passed by, and the bells of Congregational Church rang at the top of the hour. Out of the corner of my eye, I saw Kyle walking toward me.

"Congratulations," he said.

I didn't bother looking up.

"To us."

"Us?" I said.

"The state championship is ours," he said.

"Yours more than mine."

"We win as a team," Kyle said. "And you and me are teammates."

"Does it matter?" I said. "The season's over."

I picked out a pebble and flicked it toward the gutter. It bounced through the metal grate. I flicked another, but that one careened away.

"Look," Kyle said, "I was an asshole last week. I'm sorry, okay?"

He sat down on the curb opposite me. We didn't say a word for a while. Kyle grabbed some pebbles. He tossed one at the sewer. It missed. He threw another. That missed, too.

"And thanks for taking shots at Maako," Kyle said.

Disgust and disillusionment roiled inside me. All toward the guy, twenty or so feet away, who had been my best friend most of my life. Finally, I couldn't hold back any longer. I stared Kyle straight in the eye.

"I know what you did."

"What are you talking about?" he said.

"I know what you did last Saturday night."

"At the circle?" he said. "I drank too much, sure. Got a little loud, definitely. But I didn't *do* anything."

"Don't bullshit me," I said.

"I'm not."

"We've been friends a long time, Kyle."

"Yeah, and friends don't accuse each other, out of nowhere."

I shook my head. "But you're lying."

"For the sake of playing this little game of yours, let's just say I am lying. How would you know?"

"I saw," I said. "I was there."

"Where?"

"In the woods."

The color in Kyle's face disappeared and his shoulders sank. He picked up a pebble and threw it at the gutter. Then he picked up another. And another. Rapid fire. And each time he seemed to be venting more and more frustration, until, finally, he stopped.

"I didn't touch her, Jonny," he said. "I stopped before anything happened."

I stood up. "This was *Annalisa.* You knew how much I liked her."

"We had that bet," he said. "She was off-limits anyway."

"Fuck you, Kyle. You knew. And you still did that."

"It was Maako, not me."

"Stop lying!"

"You were drunk out of your mind, right?" Kyle said. "You must've been. Everyone at the circle was. And it was dark as hell in the woods, right? You could barely see a few yards ahead. With all that, you're gonna trust that you saw something happen, when I'm telling you it didn't?"

"You *hurt* her," I said.

"It was a mistake."

"It was more than a mistake."

Kyle shook his head. "Don't you think I realize that? You have no idea how it's killing me inside. I throw up everything I eat. I can't sleep at night. School's a complete waste."

"You seem fine during games," I said.

Kyle ignored me. "I can't keep a thought in my head. I feel like I'm going outta my mind." He glanced back at his house. "A few nights ago, I wake up suddenly. I thought I saw someone in the corner of my room. I look at the clock and it's like two thirty-one. I look back and whoever was there is gone."

"I have no pity for you."

"If I could do it over, Jonny, I would. But I can't."

"So, what're you gonna do now, Kyle?"

He looked at me. "What're *you* gonna do?"

"I don't know," I said.

"My life hangs in the balance, Jonny. The rest of senior year. Getting into college. Playing soccer ever again . . . This is my life we're talking about. My *life*."

We sat there, not saying a word, not looking at each other. Some time passed. Then Kyle said, "Remember in sixth grade when we were gonna see who could bat a golf ball over Ol' Man Leonard's house?"

I looked at him. "Why're you bringing this up?"

"You remember, right?"

"I guess."

Kyle had gone into his garage to find more golf balls. In a rush to be first, I hit a line drive right that shattered Mr. Leonard's dining room window. Before Kyle came back out, I ran across the street and hid behind some bushes. Within moments, Mr. Leonard burst out of his house, his face beet red. He yelled at Kyle, "Who did this? Did you do this?"

"I never said a word, Jonny," Kyle said.

"Maybe you should've."

"There was no reason to tell him—or anyone—you did it. Can't unbreak a broken window, right?"

"What's your point?"

"I took a beating for that, you know," Kyle said. "Later, Ol' Man Leonard banged on our front door. Told my dad I was the one who broke his six-hundred-dollar window and that I'd lied about it. Ol' Man Leonard wouldn't leave until my dad assured him I'd be punished. And punished I was, Jonny. Dad knocked me around a bit. Made me quit Little League. Asked what the hell was I hitting golf balls at houses for? Why didn't I tell the truth about breaking the window?"

"I don't remember any of that," I said.

"Memories are tricky," Kyle said. "But no matter how you see it, Jonny, just like the time we busted up those mailboxes and dumped them in the pond, I took one for you."

"You didn't have to."

"I didn't think about whether I had to or not," he said. "We're best friends."

"But you didn't have to."

"Saved us from spending all our snow-shoveling money on some stupid window, right? Best friends protect each other, Jonny. Don't turn on me now."

"So I should just forget what I saw?"

"You said it before; we've been best friends a long time."

"Maybe too long."

Kyle's face turned hard. "You mean that? Do you?"

I didn't answer.

"Fine," Kyle said. He stood up. "We're done, Jonny. We'll go our separate ways. Do what you want. I'll deal with all this shit on my own. But don't come crawling back to me when you find yourself back in the same place at school. You know what I'm talking about. Go back to being an Abigail Blonski. You had a view from the top. I guess you couldn't handle it."

IT WAS AFTER MIDNIGHT. I lay in bed for hours, thinking about whether Kyle had been right. Was I bailing on him? He had brought up an obscure incident in the past, but I remembered others well enough. Times when Kyle protected me, or I protected him, or when we both lied to avoid getting caught. Considering our years of friendship, how much of my loyalty did Kyle deserve?

Maybe it was best to let life move on. In a way, that's what Short Hills was about. Immense houses, buffered by huge lawns, hidden behind walls of trees and shrubs—the stiff upper lip revealing little to the outside world. Let time pass. Let memories fade. Let reputation mask any sordid occurrences that might be hiding just under the surface.

But that didn't feel right.

In truth, it seemed entirely wrong to lie comfortably under flannel sheets and a wool blanket, sheltered in this bedroom, in this house. Maybe I needed to spend time on my back sprawled out in the woods, half clothed, the late-fall wind blowing through me, with what was left of my senses scrambling to comprehend what was happening. Maybe—

I ripped the sheets and blanket off and sat up. Of all the hundreds of towns in New Jersey, why the hell did the Giannis move to Short Hills? Why not Summit? Or Springfield? Or Maplewood? Then maybe I could've somehow met her at a store in a mall. And I could have known her away from Trinity and Stephanie. Away from the circle. Away from Maako and Kyle.

And then none of this would have happened.

◻◻◻◻

I stood in the attic.

The storm had arrived. Heavy raindrops drummed the slanted roof above me. The air reeked of pine. I hated the smell. I could taste it in my mouth when I breathed in. It made me gag. With each quickening heartbeat, I felt a rush of blood spread throughout my naked body, down my arms and legs to the ends of my fingers and toes.

It was cold.

I *wanted* it cold.

Had the lightbulb above me been on, my breath would've been visible and my immersion in darkness would've been broken, and I would've shivered. But I kept my eyes shut and the light stayed off and I did not recognize the chill, so I did not feel it.

Time passed, until I could finally let my mind go . . .

I was at a playground.

A child, alone.

Out of a light mist, I walked up to a small carousel. It had once been cherry red, but after years of sun and rain and snow, the paint had faded to a dull crimson. I put my hand on the rail and pushed hard, running in a tight circle until I couldn't possibly go any faster. Then I leaped forward onto the spinning platform, feeling its invisible force try to throw me off. But I held on, until it eventually came to a stop.

Then I ran to a nearby slide. As I climbed the ladder, I heard a voice, sweet and reassuring.

"Jonathan . . ."

I peeked over the top.

There was a little girl standing in a halo of light. I climbed down the ladder and stepped toward her. Slowly, at first. Then I ran, but she wasn't any closer.

She called out to me, again. "Jonathan . . ."

I kept going until my heart hammered the inside of my chest and my legs stiffened and it felt as if my lungs would explode. Finally, I gave up and dropped to the ground.

When I raised my head, the girl was standing beside me. She held out her hand and I took it. We started walking—it felt more like we were floating—until we were standing at the edge of a creek. The girl pointed and giggled. What was it? I stepped closer, eager to see.

"No!"

My eyes begged to be closed, yet I couldn't look away. There was a lifeless body, half submerged in the shallow water. Blood leaked from the mouth, leaving a trail of pinkish red to dissolve downstream. I screamed so hard, my body shook. But no one heard me.

When I turned back to the girl, she was gone.

I was, again, alone.

Standing above the body.

Please, take me—

"Jonny?"

I opened my eyes.

"Jonny!" my mom said, panicked. Through the small attic doorway, she reached her hand in. "My God, what're you doing?"

The air was freezing. I immediately shivered. I tried to speak, but my teeth chattered uncontrollably.

"It's so cold in here," my mom said.

I wrapped my arms across my chest. My legs could

hardly move. My mom pulled me through the attic doorway, then out of the closet. She yanked the wool blanket
off my bed and draped it over me. I collapsed to the floor.
She held me tight, like she would never let go.

"My God," she said, her eyes filled with something
close to bewilderment. "What's happening to you?"

I'LL NEED A RIDE to school tomorrow," I said.

My mom nodded but didn't say a word.

She closed the door to the garage and left me alone. We hadn't talked all day about her finding me in the attic. If we ever did, I had no idea what I was going to tell her. I don't know why I was in there, naked, at midnight. I don't know why I had the visions that I'd had. It felt like I was going a little crazy, but even that sounded strange.

I taped the bottom seam of a large cardboard box. I found the three soccer balls I'd had in the basement and lying around the lawn. With a needle, I let the air out of each. In the box, I placed my cleats, the flattened soccer balls, a couple of copies of the *Star-Ledger* and the *Item* that had articles mentioning the county championship game, the notebook page on which I had kept track of all of my game stats, and our team photo taken at the beginning of the year.

The only thing missing was the copy of the ladder. Sometimes I was sure it existed. Other times, I figured it was just a hoax. It didn't matter either way. I wouldn't be going to the stacks to look ever again. Who knows, maybe I'd never visit the library again. I could make it through the rest of the year—whichever rung I hung on. Others could obsess about their place at Millburn. I wouldn't.

I closed the top and sealed it with strips of tape. On the side, I wrote with a felt pen, PERSONAL. I carried the box down to the basement, then into the storage closet under the stairs. I placed the box along the wall, then stacked a half-dozen crates on top. I moved an antique nightstand, picture frames, and boxes of my grandparents' dishes to either side and, finally, piled Lord & Taylor shopping bags filled with linens in front.

JONNY, ARE YOU AWAKE?"

My mom was knocking on my bedroom door. Her voice sounded odd. I opened my eyes. In the morning sun, red and blue lights flashed on the ceiling and walls through my window.

She opened the door and walked in.

"What's wrong?" I said.

My mom hesitated, then sat on the bed beside me. "I've got some awful news. This may be the worst thing you ever hear in your life . . . Something happened to Kyle. Something horrible."

She told me Kyle was dead.

My head shimmered and my lips quivered. I could feel my eyes welling up. All I could muster was, "Ma?"

"They found him in the creek," my mom said. "Under the bridge."

"Redemption Bridge?" I said.

She nodded.

"What happened?"

"They don't know exactly."

"When?"

"Earlier."

"This morning?"

My mom reached out and hugged me. "I'm so sorry . . ." She wouldn't let go. I didn't want her to. I asked her if I could stay in bed awhile. She wiped her eyes and said that was fine. She told me I shouldn't go to school and that she'd take the day off to stay home with me. I said, "Okay," I think.

After she left my room and closed the door, I got out of bed and moved toward the window. It had been raining. Two Millburn police cars were parked on Lake Road, and an officer, his hat tucked under his arm, was leaving the Saint-Claires' front door.

▢▢▢▢

A few hours later, the same officer rang our doorbell. My mom called me downstairs. I didn't know why. My mind was drained. I had nothing to tell him. The officer introduced himself and offered his condolences. He looked vaguely familiar—maybe I'd been in the car once when he pulled Kyle over for speeding. My mom offered the officer a chair in the living room, while I sat on the couch. He withdrew a pen and small notepad from his pocket.

"I realize it's been a difficult morning, so I won't take up too much of your time," he said. "I just have a few questions."

I nodded.

"I was told you and Kyle were buddies," he said.

"Sure," I said.

"How close?"

Before I could answer, my mom interrupted. "The Saint-Claires have lived across the street from us for years. Jonny and Kyle have been friends since the day they met. Sometimes they have disagreements—what friends don't? But they've been like brothers. This is just so sad, so hard to understand." She bent down and kissed me on the top of my head.

"Thank you, Mrs. Fehey," the officer said. "But . . ."

"I'm sorry," my mom said. "I'll let Jonny answer."

The officer turned back to me. "So, you guys had a problem recently?"

"No, we're friends," I said.

"So Kyle wasn't upset recently?"

"Upset?"

"Was he acting unusual at all?"

"No," I said.

"You're sure?"

"He just won the soccer state championship."

"Yes, I heard that." The officer gave his notepad a glance. "Maybe there was something else."

"Something else?" I repeated.

"Could've been anything," the officer said. "And I'm just throwing out these words to see if they jog your memory. Depressed . . . angry . . . guilty . . ."

"You think Kyle killed himself," I said.

"I haven't concluded anything," the officer said.

"But you're speculating."

"I'm investigating."

That was bullshit. He had something in mind. I sat back. I must've been smirking.

"This isn't funny, is it?" the officer said, calmly. His demeanor never wavered.

I shook my head. "Nope, it's not funny at all. What *is* humorous—even at this tragic moment—is the idea that Kyle would've *jumped* from Redemption Bridge. I've known Kyle a long time. I've competed with him, and against him. Everything about Kyle was winning, being the best, having people think of him as perfect. In a million years, he wouldn't have jumped."

"How do you *know?*" the officer said.

"It wasn't in his nature."

The officer looked at my mom. She turned to me.

"Maybe he was just screwing around," I said.

"What do you mean?" the officer said.

"Maybe he climbed the railing and slipped."

"At dawn on a Monday morning?"

"Could've been a dare," I said.

"A dare?"

I shrugged.

"We'll consider every possibility," the officer said.

"I'm kind of tired of the questions," I said. "I'm not even sure what the point is. Kyle's gone. Nothing's gonna bring him back."

The officer put his notepad away. He thanked my mom and me for our time. My mom held a shaky hand on my shoulder. After the officer left, I returned to the quiet darkness of my bedroom.

I'D NEVER BEEN TO a funeral before.

The St. Rose parking lot was nearly full. My mom pulled our car into one of the last open spaces. I got out and opened an umbrella, then moved around to the driver's side and held it up for her.

All morning, my mind had played tricks on me. I'd somehow convinced myself that all these people were in on an elaborately cruel prank—wearing dark suits and black dresses, crying and wiping their eyes on cue—and that we would all have a big laugh when someone finally said, "All right, we've busted Jonny's chops enough." Then Kyle would come out from behind a door, slap me on the back, and tell me he couldn't believe I'd fall for something like this.

But as my mom and I walked with other mourners along the church driveway toward the west entrance, it became entirely clear that moment would never come. Kyle's death was real. People's tears were real. It wasn't a joke at all.

I heard my mom's voice. "You okay?"

"Sure," I said, more reflexively than meaning it.

Ahead, hundreds of people, under a canopy of umbrellas, slowly passed through the entrance. I saw teachers from the high school and junior high, the principal and vice principal, Pennyweather, coaches from other sports, school staff. Those in the crowd standing among those on the middle and lower rungs of the ladder. Most of the junior class and a few sophomores, too.

Even in death, Kyle was an event.

At the doors, our teammates were lined up, shoulder to shoulder. Solomon was weeping. So were Maynard and Trevor. Brad had his face buried in Dennis's shoulder. Richie held out his arms. He and Gallo hugged. Then Richie went on to the next guy. Even Maako was there, dressed in black, standing alone. I wanted to feel comfort from my teammates. There wasn't anything that could be said, but it'd be enough to catch a guy's eye, strain a smile, then look away.

My mom and I stepped up the church stairs.

I got a nod.

A hand on my shoulder.

Then another.

"Sorry, Jonny," someone said softly.

I closed the umbrella. People moved aside, giving us a narrow passage into the nave. I looked up. The colored panes of glass at the top of the vaulted ceiling and along the walls seemed to glow. My mom and I walked down the center aisle, taking our seats in one of the front pews. I folded my hands and pressed them against my forehead, hearing muffled sobs echo in the vast chamber. My mom put a hand on my arm.

I felt as if people from school were watching me, looking to see when I cried and how often, if I cried long enough and loud enough. If I was in as much pain as I should've been.

A mahogany casket was presented before the altar. It had precise lines running end to end and brass handles spotless enough to cast a reflection—ridiculously grand for a box that was just going to rot in the ground. Why'd I notice? Because, as I sat before Kyle, with people expecting me to pour out tears, I couldn't help but notice the smallest of details as if I were a pious judge in a "best casket" contest. I didn't cry—I don't know why. So I squeezed my eyes closed until they ached.

A priest, tall and gaunt, stepped up to the pulpit.

"We are all a community," he said, his voice echoing.

"A community of friends and family, of students and teachers, of coaches and teammates . . . It is sad and tragic when a community loses any of its members. It is especially tragic when a community loses a member so young and vibrant . . . But with the love of friends and family comes hope . . . And, for that, we have gathered here today to pray before the Lord . . ."

□□□□

Afterward, my mom and I joined the long procession of black limousines and cars to Gate of Heaven Cemetery in East Hanover. It was still drizzling lightly, and the skies were charcoal gray. A tent was set up for the burial, but it was much too small to shelter all the mourners.

We sat behind Stephanie and Mr. and Mrs. Saint-Claire. Stephanie was dressed in black, but only slightly more tastefully than for school. Her eyes looked hollow, though I couldn't tell if that was from tears or makeup. I didn't see Trinity. It only vaguely surprised me that she wasn't there.

I stared at the casket, wondering how Kyle might've looked. Was he wearing a suit, or his varsity jacket? Or maybe Mr. Saint-Claire insisted he be dressed in his home whites. I didn't mean to think such macabre, inane thoughts. The truth was I was too numb to feel much of anything. I just hoped that some kind of emotion would seep back inside me as today passed into tomorrow, and as tomorrow passed into the day after that.

At the end of the ceremony, the casket was lowered into the ground.

I said goodbye to Kyle.

ALL WEEK, HEAVY RAIN FELL on Short Hills.

It seemed only appropriate.

I didn't go to school. There wasn't any point in classes, or homework, or dealing with people. My mom understood. I knew she was worried about me. She'd come up to my room every few hours like clockwork. I had the feeling she feared finding me hanging from the ceiling. I figured that was why she put a padlock on the attic door.

Our conversations were always the same.

"Hungry?"

"No."

"Thirsty?"

"No."

"If you want to talk . . ."

That didn't require a response.

I stayed in my bedroom, mostly. Sleeping a lot. On the floor. In bed. Half in the closet, half out. Sometimes I'd stare at the Saint-Claires' house. I knew Kyle would never walk out the front door again, but like the priest said, you had to have hope. So if I hoped hard enough, all of this would turn out to be one insanely horrific nightmare, and I would wake up to last month. Or last year. Ultimately, one of two things had to be right: Either I was going to see Kyle come out of his house, or this "hope" thing was bullshit.

Other people did walk in and out of the Saint-Claires' front door. Guys on the team. Pennyweather. Mr. Meiers. Most of our senior class. The Saint-Claires' relatives brought trays of food. Lake Road was crowded with cars. But by the third day, fewer people came by. By the week-end, just a handful.

Life moved on.

Our house remained quiet. I didn't turn on the radio. Or the stereo. Or the television. The phone rang every once in a while. The calls were mostly from parents who were acquaintances of my mom. I'd open my bedroom door and listen. They'd ask how I was doing, but always seemed more concerned with whether she had any idea why Kyle would've been climbing Redemption Bridge in

a pounding rainstorm early on a Monday morning. I figured most people at school, and certainly the teachers,
thought Kyle's death was suicide—the tragic result of a
uniquely talented teenager pushed over the edge by overwhelming athletic and academic pressure. Or something
just as pompously misguided.

My mom's response had become routine. "In all the
years I've known Kyle, he was a very well-adjusted young
man who came from a stable, close-knit family with two
adoring parents and a younger sister."

Once, after she hung up the telephone, I stepped out
of my bedroom and looked down the staircase.

"How're you feeling?" she asked.

I shrugged.

"I think it's time to go back to school," she said.
"Tomorrow, okay?"

I had to return at some point. My mom said the board
of education brought in a special counselor to speak to
students. Seemed like a monumental waste. I couldn't see
how some stranger was going to console me. What questions could they possibly ask? What answers would I
bother to give?

"Maybe you need to go outside for a while," my mom
said. "Get some fresh air."

□□□□

I walked down Lake Road, but I didn't go any farther than the ponds. I couldn't even look toward Redemption Bridge. It had that feeling of being hallowed—or haunted—ground. Even going to and from the funeral, my mom had driven the long way to avoid crossing it. I appreciated that.

For a while, I stood in the middle of the street, not sure what to do. In a cove opposite the dock, I saw a kid fishing. For no other reason than I felt I had to move my body, I walked onto the path toward him. As I approached, the kid raised his head.

"Catch anything?" I asked.

"Sunnies, mostly."

"What're you using?"

"Night crawlers."

I pointed to a pair of willow trees leaning over the water. "Might wanna cast it out that way. Under the branches. Don't use a bobber, though."

"Yeah?"

"A few years ago, me and a friend tossed a couple of mailboxes over—" I stopped myself. I had that pit in my gut again. Yeah, it was true—Kyle was gone. "Over there," I continued. "Hoping they'd become hiding places for catfish. I caught a four-pounder once."

"No way," the kid said. "A four-pounder?"

I nodded.

The bobber skittered across the water as he reeled in the line. He took off the bobber, stepped to the edge of the water, then pulled the rod back and cast it on a diagonal. The knot of worm plunked just underneath the willow tree branches. The kid studied the line for the slightest movement. I envied him. I envied that he could consume himself with whether or not a fish bit on the other end. It was so pointless, and yet so pure. I envied him, regretting that I might never again have a time as simple.

Jonathan . . .

My ears piqued. "Did you hear something?" I said.

"Hear what?" the kid said.

I ran up the embankment behind us and surveyed the area. But I didn't see anyone. Maybe what I'd heard was the wind whistling through the trees, or the whining sound of a car engine off in the distance.

Jonathan . . .

"Did you hear *that?*" I said.

The kid looked at me like I was crazy.

My eyes followed the shoreline of South Pond, but all I saw were nearly barren trees, one after the other. At the horizon, the setting sun broke through a seam in the clouds. Suddenly, everything came to life in a surreal way.

Vibrant green lily pads spun in circles, while the water's surface rippled and puckered one way, then the other. Above us, a flock of blue jays and cardinals left crisscrossing cobalt and red streaks in the sky, while the sun seemed so bright as to spit fire. Behind the dock, across the water, I noticed a girl sitting on the rowboat, tangled hair covering her face, a plaid skirt disheveled, her sweater smeared with dirt. The girl's hair parted slightly and her mouth curled into a wicked smile.

Then she went limp.

In an instant, everything turned grainy. I strained my eyes, but the girl seemed miles away. I took off down the path, running hard.

"Quit scarin' the fish!" the kid yelled.

I raced around the shoreline, jumping over tree roots, ducking under low-hanging branches. I tripped. Then tripped again. I came around to the open area behind the dock, ready to face whoever was there.

But no one was.

Just an empty rowboat.

I HELD THE TELEPHONE tight in my hand. "Stephanie, it's me," I said, when she picked up.

"Jonny? Why're you calling?"

"I need to talk to you."

"It's really late."

"I know."

"Over here, things are—"

"A mess, I'm sure."

"No, Jonny," she said. "They're totally fucked up."

"I wouldn't have called if it wasn't important," I said. "Something strange happened today. Really goddamn strange."

"Another time, Jonny."

"Give me just a few minutes," I said. "Please."

"You need to talk tonight?"

"Yes," I said. "We can meet out front."

"No," she said. "I don't want to have to explain to my parents. Meet me at the dock. I'll be there in fifteen minutes."

□□□□

Lake Road was blanketed in a vapor of darkness. My sneakers clicked oddly on the pavement and my ears stood rigid, straining to hear any sounds. I looked around but could see little. On a road where I had lived my entire life, near ponds where I had spent countless days fishing and throwing stones, uneasiness swept through my body. The trees were no longer familiar, the bushes no longer the playful hiding places they'd been when I was a kid.

I made my way along the path and followed that to the dock. There, I looked out over South Pond.

A twig snapped.

I turned.

"What's up, Jonny?" Stephanie stepped out of the shadows. "I was surprised to hear from you. People were calling about Kyle, offering condolences, wanting to tell us how magnificent he was on a soccer field, how much of a genius he was, how perfect he was in every way possible. But you didn't call for that, did you, Jonny?"

"This is gonna sound crazy," I said. "I saw Annalisa today."

"Annalisa?"

"It was her. I'm sure it was her."

Stephanie shook her head. "Is this supposed to be a joke?"

"I'm telling you, I saw her. Annalisa. Today."

"Where?"

"Here."

"Where?"

"On the rowboat," I said. "Sitting there."

"You saw Annalisa Gianni, my best friend, the most important person in my life. But you didn't see her at the library, did you? And you didn't see her in the back stairwell near the chemistry labs? And you didn't stand across the street from her house to catch a glimpse of her?"

I stepped back. "You knew?"

"Of course, Jonny," Stephanie said. "Now you're telling me she was here today."

"Yes."

"This afternoon."

"Yes."

"Sitting on the rowboat?"

"Goddamn it—yes. Have you talked to her? I haven't seen her since—" I stopped myself.

Stephanie walked up to me. She tugged on my jacket, lifted herself to my ear, and whispered. Her breath, like a feather, caressed my neck. "It wasn't Annalisa," she said, with a peculiar lilt in her voice. "The Giannis flew home to Arma di Taggia yesterday."

It was as if a hand had suddenly grabbed my throat and squeezed so hard I could hardly suck air into my lungs.

"Jonny-boy, what's the matter?" Stephanie said. "Something upsetting you?"

"I gotta go."

"Why?"

"You're messin' with my head."

"I wouldn't do that."

"You are."

"Don't go, Jonny-boy," Stephanie said. "Let's spend some more time together. This has been really fun."

I ran through the woods, then up Lake Road, trying to get away from Stephanie and South Pond as fast as my legs could take me. When I reached our front lawn, I hunched over, gasping for breath. I looked back down the street.

A girl stepped out from the shadows. I could see her silhouette. A skirt hung limply off her hips. She turned in my direction, then, just as quickly, vanished into the darkness.

SOMETHING HIT MY bedroom window.

A pebble.

Or a pine cone.

An empty Bic lighter, maybe.

I sat up in bed, my skin sweaty. A sour odor filled my nostrils. I pulled off my damp long-sleeved shirt and sweatpants and tossed them to the floor.

The clock read 5:17 a.m.

It was early. Way too early.

I should've stayed under the blankets—protected and safe. But I didn't. The air in my bedroom was cold, and when I got up, a chill climbed my spine. I shuffled across the floor and pushed aside the curtains.

Storm clouds filled the sky, peppering the glass with rain. Trees whipped back and forth, and, on our front lawn, fallen branches were scattered about. My skin puckered, and I shivered.

Out of the corner of my eye, I thought I saw someone dart across Lake Road. I leaned closer to the window, my breath fogging the glass. With my arm, I wiped it clear. I wondered if I was still dreaming, but was sure I wasn't. Someone was out there. Waiting for me. I could feel it.

I grabbed my jeans and a pair of socks. I put on a sweatshirt, then a second, and tied my sneakers. I checked the hallway, then my mom's bedroom, and quietly moved down the stairs. I opened the front door and stepped outside.

Lightning flashed.

A few moments later, thunder cracked.

My eyes darted back and forth. The Saint-Claires' house was dark. So were the others on Lake Road. I jumped off the front portico, crossed the lawn, and hit the street at a sprint, my sneakers slapping the wet pavement. I passed the Short Hills Club entrance, then North and South ponds. They seemed to watch me, step for step, breath for breath.

Quickly, the ponds were behind me. On a long stretch of Lake Road, I ran hard, with a purpose—like I did on a soccer field. Up ahead, the steel trusses of Redemption Bridge broke through a low-lying fog. But as my sweatshirts and jeans became drenched from the downpour, my legs began to tire and my lungs ache.

I slowed to an awkward jog.

Then a clumsy walk.

When I made it to the bridge's roadway, I hunched over, nearly breathless. Lightning ripped the sky, followed by booming thunder. I looked around. No one was there. I had a sudden sickening feeling in my gut. Below me was where Kyle had died. I walked along the railing and stopped at the metal ladder that led from street level to a small repair platform under the bridge. The fence access barrier had been reinforced. Must've been done this past week, I figured. I looked down. The rusted ladder and its cement moorings had been replaced, too.

Through the sound of pounding rain, I heard someone say, "Good morning."

I turned and faced the opposite end of the bridge.

Out of the fog, a girl walked toward me, wearing a sweater, dirty and soaked, and a plaid skirt that looked vaguely familiar. Matted-down brown hair hid her face. She seemed no more bothered by the rain than if it had instead been the brightest, sunniest summer afternoon. Then she pulled her hair back.

"Stephanie?" I said.

She leaned over the railing. "It's a long way down."

"What're you doing here?" I said.

"I could ask you the same question."

"I have no idea why," I said. "What's your excuse?"

"I like Monday mornings," Stephanie said, with a wink. "Monday mornings in the rain."

"Is that supposed to mean something?"

She smiled. Wickedly, I thought. "You know."

"No, I don't."

"I think you do."

"Stephanie, what are you getting at?"

"Come on, Jonny-boy, think," she said. "What is it you really wanna ask me?"

"I have no idea."

"I think you do."

"Tell me."

"That's no fun," she said, a teasing inflection in her voice. "Oh, okay, I'll tell you. You wanna know where I was a week ago."

"A week ago?"

"Last Monday morning," she said. "Right around now."

"You were here?" I said. "With Kyle?"

"I had to set the world straight, Jonny-boy." She smoothed the skirt down her legs. "I snuck into Kyle's bedroom. I stood in the corner, watching him sleep. For hours and hours. It wasn't the first time. As I waited there I wished with every fiber of my body that he'd taste the fear and panic and hopelessness that Annalisa did. When it was dawn, when it was time, I woke him up. 'Annalisa's at the bridge!' I cried out. 'Something's wrong with her.

She's gonna jump!' I sobbed. I quivered. It was quite a show."

"You tricked him," I said.

"Tricked?" Stephanie shrugged. "I suppose. Doesn't matter. Kyle thought he was going to rescue Annalisa; he was so desperate to redeem himself. He ran down one side of the bridge and leaned over the railing. I did, too— just to make it look good. 'Down there,' I said, pointing. Like a good follower, Kyle scaled the barrier and went down the ladder," she said, with a tone that was maddeningly cavalier. "It shimmied. The cement was crumbling, too. Near the bottom, Kyle's hand slipped. From the rain. He tried to catch another rung, but instead—oops—he fell." She gestured toward the platform below us. "Landed right there.

"Kyle looked up at me, so pathetically," she said. "He cried, 'I'm in trouble. Do you hear me? I thought you saw her down here? But there's no one.'"

I watched in bewilderment as Stephanie climbed up to the barrier. "Good thing the town had this fixed," she said. "Wouldn't want anyone to get hurt."

"Where're you going?" I said.

Stephanie tilted her head toward the stormy sky. "I kicked at the ladder . . . and kicked . . . and kicked," she said, showing how her shoe repeatedly slammed against the ladder's moorings. "A chunk of concrete broke off and hit Kyle." She giggled. "I don't think he was feeling so well after that."

"You *hurt* him?"

"Hurt? Kyle didn't know hurt. I know hurt!" Her body shuddered. "He took something away from me. Something beautiful. Something precious. Someone so vulnerable. 'I didn't mean to,' he said. 'I'm sorry.' Sorry? What good was sorry?"

"Stephanie," I said in the calmest voice I could manage.

But it was as if she didn't hear me. "Kyle showed me his hand," she said.

"Stephanie," I said, louder.

"He said it was broken—"

"Stephanie!"

She stopped, and looked at me.

"You woke me up this morning, didn't you?"

"Like I told you last night, Jonny-boy, we never spend any quality time together." Stephanie climbed back down from the barrier. "Now we are."

This was insanity. I didn't need to be out at this ungodly hour, in this shitty weather. I just wanted to be back home. In bed. Safe and warm. I'd witnessed enough tragedy for a lifetime. I'd seen things that shouldn't be seen.

I was done with Stephanie's games.

"I'm gonna go," I said. "And you need help."

"*I* need help?" She laughed. "I don't think so."

Someone walked up behind me.

I turned.

And Trinity grinned. Like Stephanie, she wore a plaid skirt and stained sweater. No black hair, no black makeup, no black pants or boots. Not a hint of goth.

I wheeled back toward Stephanie. "What the hell's going on?"

"Revenge is so very sweet, my dear Jonny-boy." She held up a pair of panties. "Recognize these?"

"No," I said.

"They're Annalisa's. Remember when she was spread out on the ground near the circle like a rag doll, while you hid and watched?"

"What are you talking about?" I said.

"Don't try that shit with me," Stephanie said. "I *saw* you there."

My throat tightened. "You saw me?" I choked out the words. "I didn't know it was her, God, I swear . . ."

"She tried to kill herself, you know," Stephanie said. "She's not the same. The Annalisa we knew is no more. Gone. Can't bring her back. So I made a promise that whoever was part of hurting her would rot in hell and never be able to forget what was done to my beautiful friend. So I ask you, Why didn't you stop them?"

"I tried to—"

"Liar!" Stephanie yelled.

"I wanted to."

"But you did nothing."

"I was wasted," I said.

"So?"

"I couldn't think straight."

"Or make a noise? Or get up? Or do any other god-damn thing?" Stephanie said. "Know what I think? I think you enjoyed watching. Bet you even got hard. Look at me. Look at me!" She pulled her fist back and swung through, connecting with my jaw.

Flash—

My knees buckled. I reached my hand out to the railing. It wobbled slightly.

"You're pitiful," Stephanie said.

I straightened up.

The two girls stepped closer.

I wiped my mouth and muttered, "Why didn't *you* do anything?"

"Oh, don't pass judgment on me," Stephanie said. "I was there too late, when it was over, when they walked away leaving her discarded in the dirt. I could only pick up the pieces." She reached her arms out like she was cradling a baby. "I covered Annalisa and held her. She didn't stop shivering. She was so cold, so exposed. Her body wasn't hers any longer; it was tainted. She whispered to me, '*Sono stanco ... Sono stanco ...*' But you, Jonny-boy, you had a chance to stop what happened. Instead, you watched my brother make Annalisa bleed. And still, you never said a word."

"I was his friend," I said. "His friend. Do you understand that?"

"His friend," she said, dismissively. "All these years you kidded yourself, following him around school like a puppy dog, wishing you could have half his talent, half his looks, half of everything he had."

"We were *best* friends."

"Silly Jonny-boy, you didn't know Kyle. You didn't know what was going on in his head. You didn't know what he was capable of."

"I was only trying to—"

"What?" Stephanie snapped. "Protect him? From the consequences of what he did to Annalisa? He did it, that's all that mattered. Just like you watched it happen and did nothing—that's all that matters. You could've saved Kyle that night in the woods. You could've saved Maako. You could've saved Annalisa. But you didn't save any of them. Look at your hands."

I did.

"Her blood is on them," she said.

I hung my head. "Please let this end."

Stephanie shook her head. "What, and just forget everything?"

"Kyle paid for what he did," I said, gesturing below us. "You sent him down there."

"Yes, and he trembled like a scared kitten," Stephanie said. "But there was nowhere to hide. He had to face me. He reached out his hand and stepped up a rung. I kicked at the cement. Again and again. He climbed a second rung. Then another. I gave the cement one last kick." She smiled. "Everything broke apart, and the ladder fell back. Kyle's hand and foot slipped off, and his body swung out wide, beyond the platform. He grabbed for a hold of something—anything . . ." Stephanie took a deep breath, seeming so pleased. "There was nothing but the wind."

"So that's how it ended?" I said quietly.

"Kyle needed to be taught a lesson," she said. "Now we'll teach *you* one."

I wiped the rain and tears from my eyes. "Annalisa isn't coming back; you said it yourself. It's over, Stephanie."

"Over?"

"Yes, over."

"It's not over."

"It's *been* over."

"No," she said. "Not yet."

I looked into Stephanie's deep, hollow eyes. She glanced at Trinity. Before I realized what was happening, both girls grabbed me by the collar of my sweatshirt, screamed like they were releasing the furies of hell, and slammed me against the railing.

But my body didn't stop. The railing gave way and I fell backwards, my arms and legs flailing wildly. In the chaotic explosion of my terrified mind, I had a final, singular moment of lucidity.

I heard Stephanie's voice.

"One more . . ." she said, a moment before my head—

High School Copes with Trio of Teen Suicides

SHORT HILLS—Little more than two weeks ago, Millburn Township celebrated its high school soccer team's victory in the Group III state title game. Today, the affluent Essex County community is reeling from the tragic news that a third member from that championship team has taken his life.

On Saturday, police discovered Erik Maako, a defensive standout, in the woods behind his home, in a scene described as ritualistic. A toxicology report isn't expected for weeks, but preliminary evidence suggests a self-administered poisoning.

Maako's death follows that of Kyle Saint-Claire and Jonathan Fehey, who fatally jumped from a local bridge, one week apart. While citing athletic pressure and adolescent angst as possible triggers, school officials were unsure of why these students would have been so affected, and why now.

"Kyle, Jonny, and Erik had tremendous skill on the soccer field and strong affection for one another that brought success to the team," said athletic director George Meiers in a statement. "They were good students in the classroom and decent kids away from school. We will remember them that way."

Meiers then announced the creation of an award, named in memory of the three teammates, to be presented each season to the soccer team's most valuable player.

That, however, is little consolation for a town that has become all too familiar with mourning the loss of its best and brightest. As the first-period bell rang on Monday morning, classmates at Millburn High crowded around an anonymous letter posted in the main hallway that seemed to capture their collective grief.

It read, in part: "A friend was recently taken away from me. Someone who was loved immensely; someone who loved back just as much. My heart cries out. No one will ever truly understand what my friend meant to me. That is the real tragedy . . ."

Author's Note

THE LATTER HALF OF THE 1970S were heady days for American soccer fans. In 1975, the New York Cosmos pulled off one of the most important player signings in sports history, luring Pele—the most recognizable athlete, if not human being, on earth—from his native Brazil. Interest in the North American Soccer League exploded, while the Cosmos instantly became the NASL's flagship franchise.

As a teen growing up a short drive from Giants Stadium, home to the Cosmos, I celebrated the team's Soccer Bowl championships in '77 and '78, and marveled at watching many of the world's greatest soccer players in a Cosmos uniform, including Carlos Alberto, Franz Beckenbauer, Giorgio Chinaglia, Vladislav "Bogie" Bogićević, Dennis Tuert, Johan Neeskens, Andranik Eskandarian, and Americans Shep Messing and Ricky Davis.

Yet it was the 1978 World Cup finals that elevated the game of soccer to ethereal heights for me. As this was before ESPN and other cable sports channels, the Internet, or any coverage on regular television, I had to wait for my issue of *Sports Illustrated* to read about Argentina's magnificent 3-1 victory over Holland. I can still remember turning to the cover story and seeing the photograph of Mario Kempes in his céleste and white #10 jersey, arms outstretched, confetti at his cleats, celebrating the first of his two goals. It was an image I would never forget.

□□□□

Over the End Line, however, is about more than just soccer. The novel touches upon serious issues that, I hope, will have the reader think about the meaning of friendship, the power of the celebrated athlete, and the interactions between teen guys and girls.

This was a difficult novel to write. I am indebted to my intrepid editor, Karen Grove, who helped draw out of me the story as I envisioned it, and who showed virtuous patience when the going was painfully slow. I also want to thank my agent, Susan Schulman, who remains a positive influence on my work, and a few of my high school soccer teammates— Jeff S., Steve H., Bill B., Bobby T.—whose memories of our practices, opponents, and on-the-field specifics were much clearer than mine. And, of course, to Alisa, Elizabeth, my sister Jennifer, and all my friends and family whom I mentioned in my previous novel, *Pinned,* I, again, offer my most sincere appreciation for your support.

Finally, I thank my mother. I could write more, but a thousand pages of words wouldn't do justice to all that she has sacrificed over the past forty-four years to allow me the opportunity to reach every goal I ever imagined. I am grateful and proud to be her son.

Alfred C. Martino
September 2008

DATE DUE

SEP 0 8 2010	